"Shiveringly gothic. . . . Watching Julia blossom away from prying eyes is almost as satisfying as seeing Jasper Blunt pine for her from nearly the first page. . . . For best effect, save this one for a windy night when trees scrape against the windowpanes."

— *The New York Times Book Review*

"Mimi Matthews never disappoints, with richly drawn characters and couples whose individual shortcomings become strengths when paired together."

— #1 *New York Times* bestselling author Jodi Picoult

"Mimi Matthews has become one of my favorite authors. She never disappoints.!"

— Mary Balogh, *New York Times* bestselling author

"No one writes Victorian romance like Mimi Matthews!"

— Kate Quinn, *New York Times* bestselling author

"Mimi Matthews just doesn't miss."

— Evie Dunmore, *USA Today* bestselling author

"Mimi is truly a national treasure. All of her books are filled with such delicious chemistry and heart, and her writing is superb. This one is another winner. Highly recommend."

— #1 *New York Times* bestselling author Isabel Ibañez

"Thrilling, poignant, and romantic . . . Mimi Matthews's evocative prose carries readers on an unforgettable adventure through London's bustling streets and elegant drawing rooms."

— Chanel Cleeton, *New York Times* bestselling author

"What I love about Mimi Matthews is that in the crowded field of historical romance, she always finds new and interesting slants for her plots and characters. That, along with her wonderful writing and meticulous research, makes every book she puts out a rare treat to enjoy and savor. Highly recommended!"

— *New York Times* bestselling author Kate Pearce

"Lush, seductive, original— *The Siren of Sussex* drew me in from the first page and wove its magic. A fresh, vibrant, brilliant Victorian romance, making it an unforgettable read."

— *New York Times* bestselling author Jane Porter

"An exquisite historical romance that is so captivating I had to force myself not to gallop through it at a breakneck speed, wanting to savor the author's obvious care and delicate attention to detail...A must read for lovers of historical fiction."

— Meg Tilly, Golden Globe-winning and Academy Award-nominated actress and author

"There are few things more satisfying than curling up with a Mimi Matthews' novel."

— Stephanie Barron, author of *The Jane Austen Mysteries*

"I've long been a devoted fan of Mimi Matthews. . . Her command of historical detail is faultless."

— International bestselling author Jennifer Robson

"This story unfolds like a rose blooming, growing more and more beautiful as each delicate layer is revealed. A tender, luminous romance. I loved it more and more with every chapter!"

— *USA Today* bestselling author Caroline Linden

"The best book I've read in a long time: gorgeously written, thoughtfully considered, swoonily romantic, and unafraid to examine issues of class, race, and gender."

— National bestselling author Olivia Dade

# Books by Mimi Matthews

The Winter Companion

***Victorian Romances***

The Lost Letter

The Viscount and the Vicar's Daughter

***Victorian Christmas Novellas***

A Holiday By Gaslight

***Victorian Romantics***

Fair as a Star

***Gothic Fiction***

John Eyre

---

## NON-FICTION

The Pug Who Bit Napoleon:

Animal Tales of the 18th and 19th Centuries

A Victorian Lady's Guide to Fashion and Beauty

# The Governess and the Rogue

## SOMERSET STORIES
### BOOK SIX

## MIMI MATTHEWS

*For Stella, who is always true.*

# Chapter One

*P.O. Steamer "Pera"*
*Alexandria to Marseilles*
*March 1858*

Beatrice Layton crossed the moonlit deck of the ship, her cheek still burning from the stinging slap she'd received. She'd be fortunate if it didn't leave a bruise. And if it did, she thought bitterly, she'd have no one but herself to blame.

Everyone from Calcutta to Bombay had warned her not to take a position as governess with the deplorable Dimsdale family. The parents were well-known tyrants, and their four children even worse. Bea had observed the little villains often over the years, shouting at their mother, striking their native bearers, and driving off one ayah, nanny, and governess after another.

When the time had at last come for the Dimsdales to quit India, there had been no one left for them to hire to look after their beastly brood on the months-long voyage home. No servant desperate enough—or stupid enough—to take them on.

Not until Bea.

Drawing her thin, knitted shawl tighter about her arms, she walked to the ship's railing just as she did every night after dark, preparing to make her obligatory wish on the evening star. It was a longstanding ritual, taught to her by her late mother. One practiced whether Bea was at home or abroad, on land or over water. She was loath to abandon it.

Not that it ever worked.

Bea had wished for countless things in the past two decades and none of those wishes had come true. That she persisted owed more to honoring her mother's memory than it did to any intrinsic faith of her own. The late Sybil Layton had believed in stars and wishes and all manner of lovely romantic things. As a girl, Bea had believed in them too.

But she was no longer a child of six. She was a woman of six and twenty, alone in the world, with only herself to depend upon. Harsh reality had long ago leached the romanticism from her soul. She'd been forced to be practical. To see things as they were, rather than wishing for some star-sent miracle to change them.

Nevertheless...

Some childhood habits were excessively hard to break.

She approached the rail of the ship, searching the sky. There was a full moon tonight. It shone as bright as a naphtha lamp, shimmering in concert with an abundance of twinkling stars. Their light was reflected in the sea below—an endless expanse of softly rippling black water that stretched, unbroken, toward the horizon.

It had been two days since Bea had seen land. And it would be many more until she saw it again.

Endless days, and every one of them a trial. And for what? For the price of passage back to England? To a country where she had no friends or family to welcome her? Where the best she could hope for was a chance to find another position?

Her shoulders slumped. She leaned against the rail, feeling the uncharacteristic prickle of tears at the back of her eyes. In moments like this, she wondered why she kept going. But she had little choice. It was either persevere in her present position, or—

A deep, masculine voice sounded behind her. "You're not thinking of jumping, are you?"

Bea's heart leapt in alarm. Spinning around with a start, she came face to face with a gentleman she'd never seen before.

But not a gentleman. A *soldier*.

He was unshaven, clad in an old wool cavalry coat and trousers, and balancing some of his weight on the cane in his right hand. It was that which first caught her attention. The rest of him came second—the broad shoulders, tousled golden hair, and weary ice-gray eyes that glinted with a trace of wry humor.

Her mouth went dry. "I *beg* your pardon?"

"I wouldn't advise it," he said. "We'd both end up drowning."

Bea took an unconscious step backward. The ship's rail pressed against her back. "*We?*"

"I'd have to leap in after you, wouldn't I?" he said. "That's what heroes do." His mouth quirked briefly. "Or so I've been told."

Her pulse accelerated as he came to stand beside her at the rail. He was a full head taller than she was and smelled, very faintly, of bay rum.

She hadn't been personally introduced to everyone on the ship, but after the land portion of the journey from Suez to Alexandria, she knew them well enough by sight. And this man—this *rogue*—wasn't among the passengers she'd seen.

He must have boarded at the docks in Alexandria, else she would have noticed him. He was the sort of man a woman *would* notice, even if she didn't have a mind to.

"You should know," he said, casting a glance out at the water. "It's not as calm as it looks from this distance. *And* it's cold. If you must throw yourself over the side, I'd advise you wait until we're nearer to Greece."

Bea drew herself up with offended dignity. Never mind that her heart was still racing. It wasn't safe to be alone with a strange man. Not when one was an unmarried woman of the servant class. And certainly not in the moonlight.

"I was *not* planning on throwing myself over the side," she informed him. "Mister...?"

"Colonel," he said. "As to the rest, I'm afraid I'm traveling incognito. I prefer to keep it that way, Miss Layton."

She blinked in surprise. "You know my name?"

"I've observed you on the deck with your young charges. They're forever shrieking it." His gaze fell to her reddened cheek. A frown darkened his brow. "Did one of them do that?"

Bea flushed, mortified that anyone, even a stranger, should witness the depths to which she'd fallen. A half dozen responses sprang to her lips—bitter, candid, ill-advised. For once, she managed to restrain them. For all she

knew, this self-described colonel was a friend of the Dimsdales. The last thing Bea wanted was to be caught speaking
ill of her employers.

"They *are* willful children," she allowed. "But—"

"They're not children at all," he said. "They're savages."

She flinched at his plain speaking.

So, not a friend of the family, then.

But not a friend of hers, either.

Bea couldn't afford to agree with him. Her position was
already too tenuous.

Turning back to the rail, she again faced the sea. The full
skirts of her plain wool dress fluttered in the wind that whispered over the moonlit water. A shiver went through her
slim frame. "Yes, well, if you must know... It's a temporary
position. I've only to endure it until we reach
Southampton."

The colonel remained at her side. "That's nearly two
weeks altogether."

Her stomach knotted. "I'm aware."

"If they're already striking you—"

"Really, sir, it's none of your affair."

"—it's only going to get worse."

She shot him a doubtful look. He sounded so certain.
"You have experience with children?"

"My siblings have been extraordinarily prolific in my
absence. Their offspring frequently write to me. I suppose
they could be little beasts as well, but I confess, they don't
seem so from their letters."

Her lips flattened in a repressive frown. "A correspondence with nieces and nephews hardly makes you an
expert."

"Not only a correspondence. I see them for short

periods whenever I'm on leave." He paused, adding, "And I'm expert enough to know that no one should be laying hands on you."

Bea privately conceded his point. "As to that... I mean to speak to Mrs. Dimsdale about it in the morning."

"If I were you—"

"Which you aren't."

"—I'd wake her now. There's no point putting it off until tomorrow. Better to confront the thing head on than—"

Bea straightened. "If you're quite finished?"

His expression hardened with impatience, but his eyes were kind. "I'm offering you the wisdom of my experience."

"I thank you for it, Mr. Colonel." Bea tightened her shawl about her. "But the hour grows late. I pray you would excuse me."

Not waiting for his reply, she turned on her heel and strode off across the deck in the direction of her shared cabin. Her pulse beat heavily at her throat. He'd flustered her, drat him. And it wasn't because he'd taken her off her guard. Or even because he was so handsome beneath his overgrown hair and beard.

It was because she'd been tempted—sorely, recklessly tempted—to confide in him.

Which would have been a mistake indeed.

Bea had learned her lesson on that score. To be sure, it was the very reason she was in this predicament. Dismissed from one post after another, for being too bold, too opinionated, too bloody difficult, until the only family left to whom she could apply for work were the Dimsdales.

Unpleasant as her new position was, Bea couldn't afford

to risk it. Certainly not by unburdening herself to an impertinent stranger she'd only met three minutes ago.

No matter that he'd seemed sympathetic. Or that his eyes had been kind.

No.

If she was going to make it through this ordeal, she must hold her tongue, keep her own counsel, and, above all, refrain from rocking the boat.

———※❦※———

JACK BERESFORD WATCHED THE PRIM LITTLE governess march off in the direction of the ship's single and double-berth cabins. She rather resembled a sparrow who'd had its feathers ruffled. She was that plain of feature, that slim and small, with severely styled brown hair and an unusually pale face.

Her drab dresses didn't help to dispel the illusion. Every time Jack had spied her on the deck she'd been clad in ill-fitting coarse brown cloth or dreary gray wool. Even so, she'd commanded his attention. There was starch in Miss Layton's spine and a vaguely stubborn tilt to her chin. It hinted at a formidable strength of will.

And Jack admired strong-willed women.

He wondered who she was underneath that starch, and what it was that made her look out at the stars with such melancholy attention.

"Sad creature," Maberly remarked, emerging from the shadows.

Jack flexed his fingers around the handle of his cane. They were cramped from all the letters he'd been writing. A frightful nuisance. One would think he'd have developed more stamina for the task. It had been his primary occupation since departing Egypt.

"Aren't we all?" he replied distractedly.

"Some sadder than others." Maberly came toward the rail. Not much more advanced than Jack's own four and thirty years, the stocky batman managed to look far older. His shock of chestnut hair had gone gray somewhere between Sebastopol and Ahvaz, and the unrelenting desert sun had turned his once youthful complexion to creased leather. "Take that burned gent in the foredeck cabin. Thornhill. Cavalry soldier, he were, rescued from a sepoy prison."

Jack knew about the fellow. The man had boarded the ship in Alexandria at the same time as Jack and several other wounded soldiers. Many were recovering from injuries suffered during the Indian rebellion, while others—like Jack—were still nursing their wounds after last years' conflict in Persia.

"None of us has escaped unscathed," Jack said.

"Leastways, he got a fine horse out of it," Maberly replied. "He has him stabled on board. A great big chestnut stallion. Hiran, he's called."

"Lucky fellow," Jack said. He'd hoped to return with a horse or two of his own. Perhaps some carpets too, and a few trunks of souvenirs. Instead, he'd barely escaped his last battle with both limbs intact.

If one could call it a battle.

"You might talk with him if you want a chat," Maberly suggested. "Safer than revealing yourself to the dogsbody servant of some jumped up colonials."

Jack felt a flash of irritation. "I've no desire for a 'chat,' as you so quaintly put it," he said. "And I didn't reveal myself."

"Beg pardon. I thought you was meant to be hiding from the ladies."

Jack narrowed his eyes at his batman. Is this what Maberly thought of him? That he was some spineless coward? "I'm not hiding from anyone."

"Avoiding, then," Maberly amended.

Jack didn't reply. He *had* been avoiding people, in truth. And the ladies in particular. But it wasn't Miss Farraday and her marriage-minded mama he was thinking about now, or any of the attractive single ladies or ripe young widows who had pursued him during his time abroad. He was thinking of drab little Miss Layton and the burning red handprint across her cheek.

His temper crackled with unexpected heat.

Someone needed to grab those Dimsdale children by the scruffs and knock their heads together before they did one of their servants permanent harm.

"Miss Farraday and her mother very nearly had you in Cairo," Maberly reminded him. "If they were to discover you're on the ship, they'd plague you night and day until they caught you good and proper."

"No one on board knows who I am, save for the captain and a handful of the crew," Jack said. "I intend to keep it that way. As for any woman catching me..." He inwardly recoiled at the thought. "I've successfully evaded a leg shackle for years. I'll not fall at the final hurdle."

"You will if you insist on chatting with unmarried women in the moonlight."

"Not a woman, a governess," Jack said. "And Miss Layton wasn't trying to beguile me." Though, he reflected, her tear-damp eyes *had* been an uncommonly pretty shade of porcelain blue. That had been beguiling in itself. "She's come out on the deck every evening since we left port."

"Just as you have," Maberly said. "Happen you'll meet her again."

Jack lapsed into silence. He'd already spent too many hours in his small cabin, devoid of company and conversation, only emerging at night to take the air. The prospect of two more weeks of isolation sat heavily on his shoulders. Especially now, when fate had presented him with an unexpected alternative to his solitude.

Given his present circumstances, the idea of encountering Miss Layton again wasn't entirely unappealing.

"Perchance I will," he replied. "What harm could it do?"

# Chapter Two

"Are you aware that there are anonymous soldiers traveling on the ship?" Bea inquired as she bent to remove her well-worn leather half boots.

Pearl turned over in her upper berth to peer blearily down at Bea in the lamplight. A petite Anglo-Indian girl with sleek black hair, she was employed as a maid-companion by Mrs. Rawson, a portly colonial dowager. Mrs. Rawson and her temperamental Maltese dog, Benjamin, had departed Bombay at the same time as Bea's employers. As a consequence, Pearl and Bea had often been obliged to bunk together, first on the voyage to Suez, then overland to Alexandria, and now on the Pera.

They weren't close in age (Pearl being several years younger than Bea), but over the past three weeks, proximity had inspired something like a friendship.

"The injured ones that came aboard in Alexandria?" Pearl asked in return. "What about them?"

"How was I unaware of their existence?"

"Because Mrs. Dimsdale keeps you on the trot from dawn until dusk," Pearl answered.

Bea stripped off her wool bodice, hanging it on one of the clothing hooks that were affixed to the small cabin's wall. Pearl wasn't wrong. Since entering the Dimsdale's employ, Bea had been run off her feet, acting as governess, nursery maid, *and* as occasional laundress. It was no wonder she'd failed to notice the presence of injured soldiers on board.

"Yes, but—" Bea stepped out of her skirts, petticoats, and crinoline. "Don't you think it odd that we don't see them?"

"Who would wish to?" Pearl asked. "Some of them are grievously injured. I heard Mrs. Farraday tell Mrs. Rawson that it's a mercy we've been spared the sight of them."

Bea winced. The widowed Mrs. Farraday was the most top-lofty lady on board, boasting both pedigree and enviable connections. She was, it was said, the daughter of a gentleman. And her own daughter—a very pretty, if somewhat insipid, girl of nineteen—was rumored to have come within a whisker of being engaged to the son of the Earl of Allendale.

Whoever *that* might be.

"What a dreadful thing to say," Bea replied.

"But the truth," Pearl pronounced.

"Her truth," Bea said, hanging up her skirts. "Not mine."

Pearl flopped over in her berth, snuggling back into her pillow. "That's your trouble. Everything is a quarrel. You'd be better off agreeing with them. It's what I do."

Bea unpinned the tightly braided coil of her hair. "I'm practicing saying nothing."

"That isn't the same as being agreeable," Pearl informed

her. "Mrs. Rawson says unwarranted silence is tantamount to insolence."

"That's because they wish to regulate every aspect of our behavior, even our thoughts," Bea retorted. Stripped down to her chemise and drawers, she went to the basin and hastily washed before dousing the lamp and climbing into her own cold berth.

There was no time to write in her journal this evening. Not that it mattered. Since leaving India, she'd had precious little to record save for the mounting indignities she'd been subjected to.

Her cheek was still stinging in grim reminder of the latest one—*and* of the task that awaited her in the morning. Like it or not, as soon as the sun was up, Bea was going to have to confront Mrs. Dimsdale about her children's behavior.

It wouldn't be the first time Bea had faced the proverbial firing squad.

During the course of her brief employment, she'd brought Mrs. Dimsdale countless complaints, all to no avail. Whatever harm her brood inflicted, the woman inevitably found a way to lay the blame on Bea's shoulders. On the last occasion, she'd even gone so far as to threaten Bea with dismissal.

Tomorrow's encounter was all-but guaranteed to be an unpleasant one.

"What do you suppose happens to servants who are sacked midway through a long sea voyage?" Bea asked.

Pearl didn't answer. She'd already subsided into sleep.

13

———————

Bea stood in front of her employer in the ship's well-appointed saloon, her back straight and her hands clasped in front of her, feeling more like a scullery maid awaiting a dressing down than a dignified governess addressing a legitimate grievance. Raising her voice, she repeated her previous sentence over the screeches of her young charges. "I said that I'd hoped to speak with you alone, ma'am!"

Mrs. Dimsdale remained seated before her. She was a faded, fair-haired woman, easily angered and overly fond of iced gin, with a hard mouth and an approaching double chin. The kind of English lady one encountered with frequency in India. She was flanked by her nine-year-old son, Albermarle Junior, and her eleven-year-old daughter, Lilith.

The two children glared at Bea in unmistakable challenge as their younger siblings—twin six-year-old boys—ran circles around the saloon, punctuating their permutations with various whoops and shrieks.

There was no one about to object to the chaos. Not at this time of morning. The other passengers had already gone into breakfast.

"And who would look after the children during this interview?" Mrs. Dimsdale asked.

"Perhaps their father—" Bea broke off as one of the twins flew past. Like his brother, he was clad in a blue flannel sailor suit. Bea had pressed the matching garments for them herself at dawn, well before tending to her own toilette.

Mrs. Dimsdale jerked the full skirts of her ruffled morning gown out of the little boy's path. "Do have a care, Brent! You'll trod on my hem."

"I'm not Brent, I'm Damian," the twin returned cheekily before galloping off across the carpet with another shriek.

Albermarle Junior's mouth curled into a sly smile. "Miss Layton can't tell them apart either," he said. "No one can."

"On the contrary," Bea replied. "That *was* Brent."

Albermarle Junior's smirk froze on his face.

"She's marked their clothes," Lilith said scornfully. "I told her she wasn't allowed to—"

"Mama!" Damian leapt by with a high-pierced cry. "Mama, look at me! See how high I can jump!"

Mrs. Dimsdale pressed her fingers to her temples. "Can you not control them, Miss Layton? All this shouting is bringing on one of my megrims."

"No, ma'am, I *can't* control them," Bea snapped back, her patience at an end. "Which is precisely why I wished to speak with you this morning!"

Mrs. Dimsdale's bosom swelled with indignation. Beside her, Albermarle and Lilith froze in unholy expectation. Their mother was known for raking her servants over the coals. And she had no great fondness for Bea. She'd only hired her out of desperation.

Bea's eyes closed briefly, knowing what was to come. She inwardly braced herself, cursing her unruly tongue.

"You will moderate your tone when you speak to me, Miss Layton," Mrs. Dimsdale commanded with bone-chilling severity. "I will *not* be addressed with impudence, no matter your complaint."

"As to that complaint, ma'am," Bea began.

*"Do you comprehend me?"*

Bea flinched. "Yes, ma'am."

"May I remind you that you're here on sufferance? Any other servant in your circumstances would be kissing my feet to have been treated with such generosity. Instead, you speak to me with disrespect and ingratitude?"

"I beg your pardon, ma'am," Bea said hastily. She affected what she hoped was a penitent manner. "But the circumstances *are* extreme."

Mrs. Dimsdale appeared even less disposed to hear of them than she had when Bea had first approached her. She gave a furious wave of her lace-trimmed handkerchief. "Well?" she demanded. "Get on with it. Or do you propose to waste even more of my morning?"

Bea clasped her hands tighter to keep from clenching them into fists. It was unjust. Unfair. All the same, it wouldn't serve her to lose her temper. "Last night," she said levelly, "when I was readying Miss Dimsdale for bed, she refused to retire. When I insisted, she struck me across the face."

Lilith flushed red. "I did not! She's lying, Mama!"

"I am *not* lying," Bea said. "For evidence, you need only consult the mark on my cheek. It is the exact size and shape of your daughter's open hand."

Mrs. Dimsdale resumed massaging her temples. "What's the use of hiring a governess if I must deal with these trials myself?" she muttered. "Am I to have no rest? No peace? Better I should dismiss you and let the children do as they will than be constantly vexed in this tedious manner."

Bea persevered. It mayn't do her any good—to be sure, she very much doubted it would—but the mysterious rogue on the deck last night had been right. Bea must draw the line somewhere. If she didn't, it would only get worse.

"I cannot perform my duties if I'm subjected to physical abuse from your children, ma'am," she said. "It is beyond all bounds."

Lilith tugged at her mother's arm. Her voice took on a familiar wheedling tone. "She was bullying me, Mama. And she *is* only a servant. I knew you wouldn't object—"

"You did strike her, then?" Mrs. Dimsdale wearily inquired of her daughter.

Lilith's face contorted. "Why should I go to bed at the same time as the babies? I'm the oldest! Papa promised—"

"God preserve me," Mrs. Dimsdale said. "My head is splitting. And I've yet to have my breakfast. Really, Miss Layton, this is not to be borne!"

"I might say the same, ma'am," Bea replied. "The seriousness of the matter—"

Mrs. Dimsdale was on her feet before Bea could finish. "You mentioned their father. Speak with him, by all means. Until such time, I would have you attend to your duties. Heaven knows they're light enough as it is."

Bea took a reflexive step toward her employer in protest. She may have brought up Mr. Dimsdale—desperately, foolishly—but the elusive gentleman was no favorable alternative to his wife. He was a hard-going colonial, consumed with shooting, drinking, and (it was rumored) the company of questionable women. Bea had never been alone with him even once since joining the Dimsdales' household.

"Mrs. Dimsdale—" she objected.

"That will be all, Miss Layton," Mrs. Dimsdale said

curtly. "The children require their morning meal. If you value your position, you will have them at the table in the next five minutes." With that, she sailed from the saloon, leaving her brood behind her.

Bea was left alone with the children, the two oldest still standing by their mother's now empty chair, and the twins continuing to ricochet around the room.

Flaxen-locked Lilith regarded Bea with a kindling eye. "You won't get any further speaking to my Papa," she informed her.

Bea's gaze fell to the child's mutinous little face. Doubtless, she was right. All the same...

Is this what Bea's life had come to? To be bested in a battle of wills with an eleven-year-old despot?

No.

*Emphatically*, no.

However bleak Bea's circumstances, there was still some fight left in her.

She looked back at Lilith. Her stomach tightened with resolve. "We shall just see about *that*, young lady."

# Chapter Three

J ack watched Miss Layton cross the deck to the ship's rail as he finished rereading his most recent letter from home. Unlike last evening, when the silver-soft moonlight had been all there was to light Miss Layton's path, tonight her pensive face and quiet figure were illuminated by the glow of the hanging lamps one of the ship's stewards had lit at sunset. As for the moon itself, it was half-hidden behind an incipient scatter of clouds.

Jack remained hidden too as Miss Layton surveyed the evening sky. It was only after giving her a moment alone that he folded his letter into the front pocket of his waistcoat and emerged from the shadows.

This time, Miss Layton didn't seem surprised by his approach.

"A fine evening," Jack said, coming to join her.

"Overcast," she replied without looking at him. "I can scarcely see the stars."

Jack followed her gaze heavenward. "Do you need to?

For navigation or some such?" He wouldn't put it past her. She was, after all, a governess. Astronomy might well be one of her subjects.

"I have no great purpose," she said. "I simply enjoy beauty. Many people do."

Jack's attention returned to her face. A drab little sparrow, he'd thought her in the moonlight. One with unusually pretty eyes. But the lamplight revealed other allurements. Those eyes were framed by elegantly winged dark brows. And what he'd yesterday mistaken in her complexion for paleness, was in fact a clear, creaminess of countenance, accentuated by high cheekbones, a well-sculpted nose, and a firmly tilted chin.

She wasn't conventionally beautiful. She was too starchy and solemn for that. But—

*The devil.*

She *was* attractive.

Jack's blood simmered with a disconcerting warmth. He brutally suppressed the reaction. It was easy enough to do for a man of his experience. He hadn't reached the advanced age of four and thirty without learning something about how to command his emotions.

"The sky will clear again," he said, a trifle gruffly. "It always does."

Miss Layton folded her arms, twining her meager knitted shawl about her. "But not tonight."

"No," he acknowledged. "Probably not."

She lapsed into silence, still staring out at the sky.

Jack regarded her for a long moment. "Let me guess," he said. "You had a frightful row with your employer about the violent conduct of your young charges, and now you find yourself in fear for your position?"

"I wouldn't call it a row," she said. "That would imply that there was an argument with two opposing sides."

"But you *did* speak to the children's mother?"

"She did most of the speaking." Miss Layton readjusted the ends of her shawl with uncharacteristically anxious fingers. "Or rather, the shouting."

Jack's brows sank with displeasure. "Don't say that she blamed you for her child's misconduct?"

"She blamed me for upsetting her peace."

"In other words—"

"In other words, there was no satisfactory resolution. The best I received was an admonishment to speak to her husband. Which is what I intend to do if I'm ever successful in running the man to ground. I've not seen him since we departed Alexandria. I'm told he spends most of his time in the gaming saloon with the other *Pukka sahibs*."

Jack gave a humorless laugh at the ironic emphasis she put on the phrase. He was no great believer in pedigree himself (his own lineage notwithstanding), but even he had to admit that the majority of his fellow countrymen who had settled in India fell short of the Hindustani expression for excellence.

Instead of drawing the very best gentlemen, India had, in recent decades, become the preferred destination for grasping men and women who had failed to make their mark in British society. Middle-class autocrats, eager to ape that very society in a foreign land, and to lord their privileged positions over that place's native inhabitants.

It was one of the many dark aspects to the expansion of Empire. One Jack had witnessed all-too-often during his years in service to the Crown. For that reason alone, he was glad to be returning home.

"What?" Miss Layton asked, hearing his dry chuckle.

"Nothing," Jack said. "Only that I don't disagree with your assessment."

"I made no assessment. I wouldn't dream of doing so."

"Your implied assessment, then." He resettled his fingers on the handle of his cane. There was a chill in the air tonight that hadn't been present last evening. Jack could feel it in the bones of his injured leg—a deep, pitiless ache. He did his level best to ignore it.

"How will you run Mr. Dimsdale to ground?" he asked.

"I sent a message to him through his valet this morning," Miss Layton said.

"And?"

She gave Jack a suspicious look. "Do you always take such an interest in solving other people's problems?"

Jack offered a vaguely apologetic smile in reply. "One of the hazards of being in charge of a brigade of men. I was often obliged to make their business my business."

"Need I point out that I'm not one of your men?"

"You may believe, ma'am," he replied gallantly, "that I could never mistake you for one."

A hint of color rose in Miss Layton's cheeks, so faint as to be practically indetectable.

Jack's mutinous blood gave a resurgent simmer in response to it.

And he wondered...

If the barest allusion to a compliment could inspire such a reaction, what result might an outright compliment have?

He was quite tempted to find out.

But no.

Jack had come too far avoiding entanglements to risk one now.

Besides, Miss Layton wasn't of his class. She didn't know how to play the game. To flirt or to tease, with no thought for the consequences. To her, all was seriousness. And doubtless it should be for one in her position.

Jack had no intention of abusing his own position for a moment's amusement at her expense, no matter how great the temptation to see the full range of her blushes.

He cleared his throat. "As to your employer—"

"With any luck, I'll hear from him sometime tomorrow," she said.

"What will you do until then?"

"What *can* I do, other than keep on managing the children?" She paused, adding, "And hoping that the threat of their father will be sufficient to keep them in check."

"It never worked for me," Jack said.

She looked at him again, this time with something like curiosity. "Your father was similar to Mr. Dimsdale?"

Jack refrained from replying that his father was similar to no other man in this world. A formidable fellow—fierce, proud, occasionally ruthless. The kind of gentlemen that Jack and his two older brothers had looked on as something like a God when they were children. A loving God, at that. There was nothing Jack's father wouldn't do for his family.

"I've not yet met Mr. Dimsdale," Jack said.

"Or anyone else, I presume," Miss Layton replied. "Since you're traveling incognito." Her voice held a hint of reproof.

Jack shrugged. "I observe people."

"From the shadows?"

"An eye-opening experience. It's how I first spied you."

Her gaze narrowed with feminine censure. "I don't care to be spied upon, sir."

He looked back at her steadily, registering her ramrod straight spine, her stiff jaw, and the resolute set to her thin shoulders. Any other gentlemen would have offered his apologies and withdrawn. But Jack was too well-acquainted with prickly females to let a few harmless barbs pierce his skin.

"It wasn't my intention," he said. "You simply crossed my path when I was taking the air. The first several nights after we left port, I thought it better to leave you alone. It was only last night that I dared approach. You appeared in some distress—"

"Indeed, I was not."

"And I— Well." His mouth quirked. "I was desperate for human contact, wasn't I?"

She gave him a reproving glare. "Ridiculous," she said. "You're not unsuitable for company, you know. Not as far as I can see."

"Thank you."

"I meant that you needn't spend your days hiding in your cabin. Your injuries don't appear terribly offensive."

He affected an eloquent wince. "Not terribly offensive? Talk about damning with faint praise."

Miss Layton didn't rise to the bait. Her countenance remained as serious as a scholar. "How did you hurt your leg?" she asked. "Was it in battle somewhere?"

Jack's smile faded. "My horse fell on me during a skirmish," he answered bluntly. "A too-green field surgeon exacerbated the damage. I was obliged to have a second surgery to repair his work. Once it heals, I'm assured I shall be as good as new."

That's what the surgeon in Cairo had said anyway.

Jack wanted to believe him, but after so many weeks of pain, doubt had begun to set in. And not only about his future mobility.

More and more Jack was realizing just how little of himself remained after the ordeal he'd been through. The agonies of multiple surgeries. The loss of his men, and his own sense of purpose.

Even the old reckless impulses had gone. Those long-ago urges that had compelled Jack to engage in all sorts of ill-advised stunts and schemes. His time in the army had blunted the lure of such temptations, but it wasn't until after he'd woken up in the field hospital that day outside of Mohammerah that they'd gone completely.

Jack didn't know quite who he was without them.

"And I'm not hiding," he added for the second time in as many days. "I'm merely avoiding unpleasant company."

Miss Layton's brows lifted. "You know someone on the ship?"

"Several someones. They would inevitably make the remainder of my voyage a misery." His fingers curled tighter around the handle of his cane. "It doesn't signify. I'm quite content taking my meals in my quarters."

Miss Layton's gaze betrayed a flicker of sympathy. "It must be dreadfully dull."

It was.

Oh, but it was.

Jack was a man of action, not quiet contemplation. He'd rather be out riding in the open country, playing cricket with his brothers, or going several rounds at his favorite boxing saloon. To huddle in that measly cabin all day, poring over old correspondence and drafting letters to send at the next port of call, was minute-by-minute eating away at his sanity.

"I have tasks to occupy myself," he said. "Letters and so forth."

"Oh?" Her attention fell to the deck. "Is this one of them?"

Jack glanced down. His letter had fallen from his pocket. The wind loosed the pages, scattering them across the boards. Before he could make a reply, Miss Layton sank gracefully to retrieve them.

He suppressed a scorching flare of aggravation.

He'd been adapting to his new limitations as best he could since leaving hospital in Cairo, but the fact that he couldn't yet easily bend his left knee to crouch or to kneel was still a source of frustration to him. He nevertheless moved to assist her, his efforts made awkward by his cane. "Allow me—"

"I have it," she said, swiftly collecting the pages. There were four altogether, covered front and back in a neat, even penmanship that had, over the past fourteen years, become all-too familiar to Jack.

Miss Layton assembled them into order and, rising, handed them back to him. "Here you are."

Jack took them, feeling as useless as he frequently did these days. "Thank you," he said stiffly.

"Not at all." Smoothing her skirts, Miss Layton returned to her position at the rail. "I wasn't aware there was any way of receiving one's post after leaving port. Not until we reached Malta."

"It's not a recent letter." He shoved it back into his pocket, more firmly this time. "I received it before leaving Alexandria. It's one I often re-read."

"A letter from a lady?" she asked with deliberate nonchalance.

Jack's smile slowly returned. "As a matter of fact," he said. "It is."

BEA INWARDLY WITHERED AT THE SIGHT OF HIS amusement. She could have kicked herself for inquiring. What did she care that he was poring over a letter from a lady? A letter written in a straight, elegant hand, covering four pages of paper. One he'd read over and over again.

A letter from someone named Hannah.

His sweetheart, Bea gathered.

Naturally he had one. What soldier didn't? Especially a soldier with roguishly handsome looks and an equally roguish manner? He was just the sort of man young ladies would be chasing after in droves. A catch, and no question, particularly if he was indeed a colonel.

"It's no business of mine," she said quickly. "Forgive my mentioning it."

"Not at all," he said. "It's no great secret."

"Yet... It must be important to you for you to have reread it so many times."

His smile reached his eyes. The icy-gray depths twinkled with humor. "You might say that. The lady who wrote it has a talent with words. It makes her letters entertaining, as well as informative."

"How nice," Bea managed. She set her hands on the cold ship's rail. She wished she'd remembered to put on her gloves before venturing from her cabin. Without them, her bare hands were revealed in all their careworn glory. The red knuckles, callused fingers, and roughened skin. Decidedly *not* the hands of a lady. Not even the hands of a governess. Not anymore.

That role had diminished year-by-year since her arrival in India. With every unsuccessful posting she'd been reduced—accorded less privilege, less respect, less money— even as her duties had increased.

The colonel drew closer to her. "You must have letters you enjoy rereading from time to time."

"Indeed, I do not," Bea said. "A governess isn't permitted to have followers."

"What about friends?" he asked. "Surely you have some of those worth corresponding with?"

Bea hadn't imagined she could feel any worse this evening. "I keep a journal," she admitted.

"Ah," he said.

The single syllable could have meant anything.

Bea forged ahead. "I've made a historical record of my time in India. And of the British occupation there. It's a fairly thorough account."

"Yet not the same thing as a correspondence with a friend," the colonel pointed out.

"I'm not... That is, I haven't..." She paused. "My positions have been such that I could make no lasting connections."

"I don't see why—"

"I've had over two dozen postings," she blurted out.

The colonel couldn't conceal his surprise. "*Two dozen? At your age?*"

Heat threatened to creep into her cheeks again. Bea refused to allow it. She was aware she looked younger than she was. But the fact remained that she was *not* young, neither in years nor experience. She was, by any objective measurement, rapidly approaching spinsterhood. "I am six and twenty, sir," she said. "Very nearly seven and twenty."

He stared at her.

Bea had to steel herself not to squirm under his regard. "It's nothing to the point," she said. "I came to India when I was but seventeen, not long out of school. Since then, I've been all across the continent, from Calcutta to Bombay, Kashmir, Hyderabad, and back again. It's not an easy life."

"Even less so, I imagine, now you're in the Dimsdales' employ," he said.

"A temporary position, as I told you yesterday. I only took it to secure passage back to England."

Indeed, some might argue that all Bea's positions had been temporary positions. She never kept them for long. One-by-one they all came to a swift end, either through mutual agreement or by courtesy of the firing squad.

"Everyone else was leaving after the uprising," she continued. "Given my diminished employment prospects, I thought it wise for me to do the same."

The colonel studied her face. "I trust you're returning home to be with your family?"

"I have no family," Bea said. Her conscience gave an immediate twinge at so bleak a statement. The conversation had taken an unfortunate turn toward the melancholy. "I'm returning to England to find a new position. Mrs. Dimsdale has promised me a glowing reference in exchange for my services."

The silence that met her statement held a wealth of unexpressed opinion. Pity, disbelief, judgment. Or, very probably, all three.

Bea folded her arms tighter about herself, feeling very much alone. "Are you?" she asked finally.

"Am I what?" the colonel returned.

"Going home to your family?"

An odd look crossed his face. "After a fashion." He half leaned against the rail beside her. "Most of my relations reside in the West Country. I own a small estate there as well. Marston Priory. My brother has had the management of it while I've been away. I plan to settle there for a time, until I decide what I'm to do with the remainder of my life."

Bea didn't know quite how to respond. It was such an abundance of riches. And ones averred to so casually. An estate. A brother. A *family*.

She should be so fortunate.

Instead, she had no one and nothing at all.

Her precarious mood dipped further. Tonight was proving to be a disappointment in every regard. First, no stars. And now, an unwelcome reminder that she had no beau, no friends, no home, no family.

She was beginning to regret ever coming onto the deck this evening. Better she had gone straight to bed.

"What do you wish to do?" she asked with mechanical civility.

"I don't know," the colonel said. "Recover my health? Write my memoirs? Breed racehorses?"

"You're spoiled for choice."

"I suppose I am."

"It must be nice."

His smile took on an edge. "Must it?"

"Whatever you decide, your family will be there waiting for you."

"What about you?" he asked. "There must be someone in England who will be eager to have you back again."

"Not a single soul." Bea belatedly realized how pathetic she sounded. "Never fear," she added bracingly. "I shall make my own way."

"I don't doubt it, Miss Layton," the colonel said. "But take care. We all need someone sometime."

## Chapter Four

Bea held tight to Brent's small hand as she and the children navigated the crowded deck the next morning. The weather was less than ideal for a promenade, but the roar of the wind and the crash of the churning sea were no deterrent to the passengers. Not when the sun was shining so brilliantly. And certainly not for Bea.

The Pera had no formal schoolroom. Given the children's bottomless wells of energy, she'd long concluded that most days during their long voyage were better spent out of doors.

"Why is Damian allowed to run?" Brent demanded, seeing his identical brother trot ahead.

"He is *not* allowed." Bea extended her free hand to the errant twin. "Damian? Here, if you please."

Damian slowed just long enough for Bea to catch up with him. He grudgingly took her outstretched hand. "This is no fun," he grumbled.

Albermarle Junior stalked beside them, hands thrust into the pockets of his short pants. "Miss Layton wouldn't know fun if it bit her in her backside," he said beneath his breath.

Bea directed a stern look at the boy. "Enough of that," she said. "You would do well to set an example for your brothers."

"What do you know about it?" Albermarle Junior retorted. "My brothers and I should have a tutor, not a nursemaid."

Lilith giggled. "A nursemaid," she echoed gleefully, twirling her parasol over her shoulder. The delicate lace canopy bowed in the wind. "That's Miss Layton to a nicety."

"I said enough," Bea repeated firmly. "You may resume reciting your multiplication tables."

Lilith's expression soured. For her, mathematical exercises were akin to a punishment. "I don't know why I must. I have no need of them."

"Every young lady has need of them," Bea returned. "And every wife and mother too. When you have a household of your own, it will be left to you to oversee the accounts and to balance the ledgers. How do you propose to do that without a thorough education in addition, subtraction, and multiplication? You were on fours, I believe."

Lilith's lower lip crept out in a final show of rebellion, even as she resumed her recitation. "Four times two is eight," she said. "Four times three is twelve. Four times..."

Bea listened, offering assistance as needed, as she and the children passed from the ship's bow to its stern. Sea air billowed over the deck in gusts, whipping at their clothes and hair.

When Lilith had finished, it was Albermarle's turn, and then Brent's and Damian's, the older children offering help (if somewhat uncharitably) whenever the younger ones faltered.

It wasn't book learning, imparted in a stuffy classroom with desks, slates, and primers. But Bea had been taught that a governess should never instruct from a book alone. To engage the rational mind of a child, a governess must excite their imagination too.

"Well done," Bea said. "What about those chairs? How many of them are there, Brent?"

The little boy took a painstaking accounting. "Twelve," he answered at last.

"And what happens if the steward were to take five of them away?" Bea asked. "How many chairs would remain? Albermarle Junior?"

"Seven, of course," Albermarle Junior replied pettishly.

"And if another steward added back ten? Lilith?"

The little girl turned to examine the water, refusing to reply.

A seagull squawked from one of the masts overhead. Another answered. The high-pitched cries were coupled with the roar of the sea and the swell of conversation around them.

Bea had to raise her voice over the din. "Do you require my help in working it out?" she asked.

Lilith jerked her head back with a scowl. The ribbons on her leghorn bonnet danced in the wind. "It's seventeen, obviously," she pronounced with dripping disdain.

"Excellent," Bea said.

"Tedious," Lilith retorted. "I prefer to practice my French."

No doubt she did. It was Bea's weakest subject. "And we shall," Bea said. "Later."

Lilith came to an abrupt halt. A crowd of ladies stood nearby, conversing beneath the protection of the ship's awning. Among them were Mrs. Rawson, Mrs. Farraday, and Mrs. Farraday's raven-haired daughter, Rowena. The latter wore a fashionable, braid-trimmed skirt and jacket, looking far more beautiful than any female had a right to look during a long voyage at sea.

"Naturally, he was the handsomest gentleman in Cairo," Mrs. Farraday was saying. She was dark-haired like her daughter, with equally dark eyes and a sharp blade of an aquiline nose. "That's never been disputed. But then, his father is famous for his handsomeness. And his brothers too. They are, on the whole, an exceptionally good-looking family."

Mrs. Rawson chuckled. A heavyset elderly woman, she was distinguished by the copious jewels that adorned her person, and by the overfed Maltese dog she carried tucked under one arm. "A rich one too. Your daughter would have been very well looked after had she managed to secure an offer from him in Cairo last year."

"All is not lost," Mrs. Farraday said. "My Rowena's beauty will yet win the day."

Lilith shot the ladies a calculating glance from beneath her parasol.

Bea's stomach sank. She knew that look. And it wasn't inspired by the ladies' conversation. It was inspired by the mere fact of their presence. Taken altogether, they provided the exact thing that Lilith Dimsdale was seeking. An audience.

"Not later!" Lilith raised her voice, punctuating her words with a stamp of her booted foot. "Now!"

"Lilith," Bea began. "This is neither the time nor the—"

"I will *not* be addressed with impudence!" Lilith interrupted in a fair imitation of her mother. "You weren't brought with us to teach us math. You're a governess! Governesses teach French. Don't you know French, Miss Layton? *Parlez-vous français?*"

The group of ladies abandoned their conversation to turn and stare.

Bea stifled a surge of mortification. "Young lady," she said quietly. "You're causing a scene. If you don't cease this instant, I shall—"

"*Tu comprends?*" Lilith continued. "*Imbécile!*"

The ladies tittered with amusement. All except for Miss Farraday. She only smiled. Detaching herself from the others, she glided toward them.

"Bravo," she said to Lilith. "*Tu parles très bien français.*"

Lilith beamed back at her with near angelic innocence. "*Merci, Mademoiselle.*"

"Perhaps you might walk with us until luncheon?" Miss Farraday suggested. "We could practice our French phrases together. If your governess will permit?" She looked to Bea. "I would be happy to return her to the dining saloon afterward."

Bea held tight to the twins' sweaty hands. Under other circumstances, she'd have resented the challenge to her authority. But Miss Farraday's interference appeared kindly meant.

That didn't prevent Bea from feeling a stab of self-consciousness. Her drab wool dress and severely plaited coiffure stood in sharp contrast to Miss Farraday's fashionable ensemble.

"She may," Bea said. "If she behaves herself."

Lilith reddened. "I don't require her permission," she

told Miss Farraday as they joined the other ladies. "My mother says that…"

Bea remained standing with the boys, hearing Lilith's words drift off as she and the ladies strolled away, and marking the laughter that followed. Her face went hot with embarrassment.

This was what she'd become. An object of derision. A person to be struck. To be laughed at.

Oh, why had she ever taken this job with the Dimsdales! Better she had stayed in India. At least there she'd have had her dignity.

But dignity was poor recompense when one was without food and lodgings. When one was starving, destitute, alone.

Brent tugged at her right hand. "Come on!"

Damian pulled at her left one, directing her attention upward to the birds that were circling the ship en masse. "How many seagulls are in the sky, Miss Layton? Can you count that high?"

"In French?" Albermarle Junior suggested.

"No more math today," Bea said. "We shall turn our attention to botany."

"No!" Brent protested.

"We're at sea," Albermarle Junior said. "There are no trees or plants to examine here."

"There are potted palms in the grand saloon," Bea said. "Those will suffice for our lesson."

AN HOUR AND A HALF LATER, AFTER DEPOSITING the three boys in the dining saloon, Bea had just enough time to return to her shared cabin to make herself fit to join them. Pearl was already there, doing the same.

"I tore my stockings crawling under the bed to fetch Mrs. Rawson's sewing bag," Pearl said as she rolled on a fresh pair. "Goodness knows how it got there. I suspect Benjamin must have carried it off." She glanced at Bea. Her eyes widened. "What happened to you?"

"The twins pressed their muddy hands all over my skirts during our botany lesson." Bea wet a sponge in the basin to clean away the dried dirt. "And my plaits weren't equal to the wind on the deck. I appear as though I've been caught in a hurricane."

Pearl stood to assist her. "Let me," she said, setting to work on Bea's hair.

"I can manage."

"Rubbish. We both know you're only given ten minutes to eat. It'll be five minutes now you've had to set yourself to rights. And no minutes at all unless I help you." Pearl speedily re-plaited Bea's tangled locks, securing them in a neat coil at her nape. "There. All done."

"Thank you." Bea flashed her a grateful smile as she finished sponging her skirt. It was damp now where the mud had been, but taken altogether a wet skirt was preferable to a filthy one.

"Have you talked to Mr. Dimsdale yet?" Pearl asked, crossing to the door.

"Not yet." Bea tossed the sponge into the basin. She hadn't time to rinse it. Not if she hoped to eat. Giving her skirts a final shake, she followed Pearl out of the cabin. "I can do nothing until he summons me."

"So long as you do *something*," Pearl said.

Bea gave an unladylike snort as the two of them hurried toward the dining saloon. "This is a fine change. Aren't you the one who's always advising me to bite my tongue?"

"There's a time for remaining silent and a time for speaking out," Pearl replied sagely. "And when one's betters start striking one in the face, one had best speak up before they get struck again."

———— ✦ ————

JACK RAPPED ONCE MORE ON THE CABIN DOOR. There was still no answer. "Stubborn fool," he muttered.

He knew Captain Thornhill was in there. The man's valet had emerged only moments before Jack's arrival, ostensibly to fetch his master's dinner tray. Thornhill had shouted something to him as he'd exited the cabin.

Not that it guaranteed the infernal fellow would willingly talk to anyone else. During the course of their voyage, he'd proven himself to be more of a hermit than Jack was.

It didn't dissuade Jack from his course. Indeed, over the past several days, Thornhill's plight had been weighing on Jack's mind with increasing frequency.

He may not be one of Jack's men, but Thornhill was still a soldier. One who, since departing Egypt, had yet to emerge from his cabin even once. At this stage, he must be half-mad with boredom. Either that or melancholy.

Jack rapped a final time, purely as a courtesy, before taking matters into his own hands. "I'm coming in," he warned.

Opening the door, he found Thornhill sprawled in a

chair in the corner of the darkened cabin, a glass of spirits dangling from his fingers. He was only partially dressed, clad in dark trousers and a shirt with the collar gaping open to reveal the angry red burn scars that traveled from his face all the way down to his chest.

A gruesome sight. But no more gruesome than the countless other terrible injuries Jack had seen during his years in the army.

Thornhill leveled an unreadable look at Jack as Jack entered. The two of them had met briefly on the docks in Alexandria. They'd both been boarding the ship well in advance of the other passengers, eager to avoid company, though not, Jack suspected, for the same reasons.

"Colonel Beresford," Thornhill said flatly. "I don't recall inviting you in."

"Didn't you?" Jack closed the door behind him, consigning them both to the shadows. "My mistake."

Thornhill took a drink from his glass. The pungent smell of the medicinal salve used to treat his burns permeated the room. "What do you want?"

Jack limped across the cabin to take an uninvited seat on the edge of the lower berth. "To see how you're doing in here," he said. "And to urge you to trade your solitude for a breath of fresh air."

Thornhill made no reply.

"You've not left your cabin since we set out," Jack said.

"I have," Thornhill informed him.

"I haven't seen you above deck."

"I go below deck," Thornhill said. "To see my horse."

Jack shouldn't be surprised. Maberly had said that Thornhill's horse was an exceptionally fine specimen.

"You might try coming topside too," Jack suggested.

"There's no one around after dark, save for an impetuous soul or two staring at the stars. It's when I go out for some air. You're more than welcome—"

"No thank you." Thornhill resumed drinking. "If that's all?"

Jack's jaw tightened. Drat the man and his obstinacy! Didn't he want to be helped?

But Jack already knew the answer. He could see it in Thornhill's eyes. He was a captive to his own misfortune. A lost soul who had already given up.

Looking at him, Jack saw the distorted mirror image of his own misery. The way he'd felt after the events at Mohammerah. As though his identity had been stripped from him, leaving nothing behind but the pain and difficulty of an existence that had been thrust upon him without his consent.

In the aftermath, Jack had become someone he didn't recognize anymore. An earthbound old man, shackled to his limitations. One who was no longer free to behave rashly. To accept a wager or levy a challenge. To feel his blood pumping in his veins as he rode too hard, swam too far, and dared too much.

He ran a hand over the back of his neck. "I'm going mad in my own cabin," he confessed. "And that's with my evening rambles to offset my confinement. I can only imagine how much worse it must be for you, hidden away in here all day, even if you *are* venturing belowdecks after dark."

"I have no complaints," Thornhill said. "Compared to a sepoy prison, this cabin is a paradise."

Jack winced at the reminder of what Thornhill had suffered. "You've been through a great deal, I don't doubt.

But if you mean to see your way out of this—"

"*This*," Thornhill repeated. "And what might *this* be?"

"Your experience," Jack said. "These wounds. Whatever it was that happened to you during your imprisonment. If you have any hope—"

"I don't," Thornhill said. "And I've no interest in fresh air, or mingling with the other passengers, or your company."

"My company is negotiable. But as to air—"

"I'll have plenty of air in Devon."

Jack's brows lifted. "Devon? Is that where you're bound for?"

"It is," Thornhill said.

Jack refrained from asking if he had anyone waiting for him there. He'd learned his lesson with Miss Layton. Not everyone had a big, boisterous family eager to welcome them back into the fold. There were many in the world who walked alone. Some by choice. Others, less so.

"To rest and heal, I presume," he said instead.

"Something like that."

"Under the care of...?"

"My attorney." Thornhill lifted his glass back to his lips. "If that's all, Colonel?"

Jack rose from the berth with the aid of his cane. He had no illusions about how differently this conversation would be playing out if he didn't outrank the captain. That Thornhill had tolerated his high-handed interference thus far was entirely owing to Jack's superior position in the hierarchy to which they'd both pledged their lives.

But even rank had its limits.

"Very well," Jack said. "I'll leave you in peace."

Thornhill didn't respond. He merely resumed drinking,

retreating into whatever grim reflection had been occupying his mind when Jack had first burst in on him.

Frowning, Jack exited the cabin. Returning to his own, he was struck by a harrowing realization. *This* was what his future held for him if he didn't alter his course. A future as an old soldier consumed by former miseries and present suffering. One who could never again hope to reclaim the identity he'd lost on the field of battle.

Jack couldn't accept it.

He *refused* to accept it.

Something was going to have to change.

The only question was what.

# Chapter Five

As luck would have it, Bea didn't cross paths with the elusive Mr. Dimsdale until much later that night, long after the dinner hour had passed and she'd put the children to bed. She was alone on the deck in the moonlight, having just made her wish on the evening star, when the fine hairs on the back of her neck lifted, warning her that someone was approaching.

This time it wasn't an unshaven rogue of a colonel. It was another man, one stinking rather heavily of whiskey.

Gathering her courage, Bea turned around, coming face-to-face with Mr. Dimsdale.

Her pulse skittered with feminine apprehension.

She may not have spent any time with Mr. Dimsdale since entering his family's employ, but she knew him well enough by sight. She'd seen him often over her years in India, shouting at native bearers, riding hard during polo matches, and striding about various encampments with similar-looking Englishmen. All of them loud, strapping fellows, with heavy beards, and weathered skin.

*Pukka sahibs.*

Bea wasn't overly fond of the breed. "Mr. Dimsdale." She inclined her head. "Good evening."

"Miss Layton." His thick lips curled in an oily smile. "What do you mean by wandering the deck at night on your own? Not waiting for me, are you?" He advanced on her. "My valet said you required my ear."

Bea had to steel herself from retreating. She'd encountered drunken men before, but never in the role of employer. "I required a breath of fresh air," she said. "But yes, I did hope that I might speak with you about the children. Mrs. Dimsdale recommended it."

"Did she, by God." He came to the rail. His gait was markedly unsteady, made more noticeable by the roll of the deck beneath his feet. "What are they up to now, the rascals?"

Bea saw no point in beating about the bush. "Your daughter struck me last evening."

Mr. Dimsdale's bushy brows lifted. "Little Lilith?" He guffawed. "I can't believe it. Not unless she was mightily provoked."

Bea's chest tightened with indignation. "There was no provocation, sir. I was merely attempting to put her to bed."

He gave another chuckle of amusement. "Is that all?"

"It was enough. You must be aware how difficult the children can be."

"I'm aware how lazy servants are. Can't get a decent Ayah or bearer wallah for any sum. Have to keep after them with the boot or the strap. That's what my children are used to, giving a bit of the old encouragement to an indolent domestic."

Bea's lips compressed. She had witnessed just such

despicable behavior, long before she'd entered the Dimsdales' employ, as had everyone else who'd encountered them
in India. It was the very reason Mrs. Dimsdale had been
unable to find a governess for her children after their last
one had unceremoniously departed.

"An unfortunate habit," Bea said, "and one that should
never have been tolerated in the first place. No one has the
right to strike a person they perceive as being beneath
them."

Mr. Dimsdale's smile dimmed. "Lofty opinions for one
in your position." He drew closer still. The stink of whiskey
and tobacco that came with him was nearly overpowering.
"Where did she strike you?"

Bea made an effort not to inhale. "On my cheek. But
that's beside the point. I would have you address her
behavior before—"

"Here?" Mr. Dimsdale's brought his hand to her face.

Bea recoiled from his touch. "If you wouldn't mind—"

His tobacco-stained fingers curved to cup her cheek,
arresting her speech and preventing her from retreating.
"What soft skin you have," he said. "One wouldn't know it
by the sharpness of your tongue."

Bea's blood ran cold. Good lord. Just how intoxicated
was he? "Mr. Dimsdale, really," she protested. "You must
desist."

His fingertips pressed hard into the curve of her jaw.
"And those pretty blue eyes. Quite fetching in the right
light."

Bea's heart beat an erratic rhythm in her breast. She was
rapidly losing control of the situation.

If she'd ever had it in the first place.

"My wife would prefer to sack you," he said, still

holding tight to Bea's face. "I expect she will after this latest episode with Lilith. No lady desires to be reprimanded by her servant. But I might put in a word for you, providing I get something in return."

Bea was left in no doubt of his intentions. Staring up at his inebriated face, her future as the Dimsdales' governess flashed before her eyes. She was a hair's breadth away from being dishonored. Either that or dismissed.

Of the two, she knew which she'd prefer.

She jerked her head back. "Unhand me this instant!"

"And what will you give me for it?" he asked. "How about a kiss? Or is that mouth of yours reserved for scolding my wife and children?"

"I said, *let me go*, you philistine!" Bea raised her hands to his chest. She was just about to shove him away with all her might when the hard clack of a walking stick sounded on the deck behind them.

"Lovely night, isn't it, Miss Layton?" a deep male voice interjected.

Bea's gaze lurched to the colonel's. A flare of unimaginable relief went through her.

It was short-lived.

Though he was dressed in the same old cavalry coat and trousers he'd worn on the previous occasions they'd met, and though his hair and beard were just as overgrown, there was something in the colonel's face so markedly different as to send a chill down Bea's spine.

It was his eyes, she realized. They were no longer kind. They were as cold as hoarfrost on a godforsaken moor.

Mr. Dimsdale abruptly released Bea's cheek. He stepped back, with a cough. "Er, I say, Miss Layton. Do you know this chap?"

Bea pressed a hand to her corseted midsection. Her breath seemed to have jammed up in her chest, and her skin had gone into some queer sort of clammy flush. She didn't know how she managed to keep her countenance.

"Colonel, may I present my employer, Mr. Dimsdale," she said. "Mr. Dimsdale, this is Colonel..." She faltered. "Colonel..."

"Beresford," the colonel replied as he came to join them. "Lately of Her Majesty's Army in Persia."

"Beresford," Mr. Dimsdale repeated with a dubious sniff. "Don't recall the name."

The colonel held Mr. Dimsdale's gaze. "You might be better acquainted with my father," he said. "The Earl of Allendale."

# Chapter Six

J ack hadn't planned to reveal himself to anyone on the ship, least of all to a half-drunk colonial.

But needs must.

An expression of astonishment spread over Mr. Dimsdale's face. It was one Jack had frequently seen before. The name of John Beresford, Earl of Allendale, often inspired such a reaction. Jack's father was both wealthy and powerful, as well as being one of the largest landowners in the West Country. He was also a gentleman known far and wide for his ruthless temperament.

A temperament, many people claimed, that his children had inherited. His ice-cold heir, James. His firebrand of a second-son, Ivo. His dauntless daughter, Kate. And his wild, neck-or-nothing youngest son, Jack, who had departed England fourteen years ago to fight for Queen and country.

Dimsdale's throat bobbed on a swallow. "The Earl of Allendale you say?" he managed. "And, er, he's your father?"

Jack felt the weight of Miss Layton's stare. Doubtless he'd shocked her too. It wasn't his foremost concern at the moment. "He is," Jack replied stonily. "And like him, I don't approve of gentlemen in your condition inflicting themselves on ladies."

Dimsdale turned red as a beetroot. "Look here," he said. "This woman's a member of my household. My children's governess. I—"

"Which makes your actions this evening that much more reprehensible," Jack said. "If this lady is indeed a member of your household, you're responsible for her wellbeing."

Dimsdale drew himself up with unsteady authority. "Exactly so. Which is why—"

"It didn't appear to me that you were looking after her welfare," Jack interrupted. "Quite the reverse." He turned to Miss Layton. "Are you all right?"

Miss Layton's chin was upraised and her shoulders squared. "I'm well, thank you."

Despite her brave face, Jack couldn't fail to notice the thready quaver in her voice.

The man had frightened her. And not only because of what he'd been about to do, but because of who he was. Unless Jack was mistaken, Miss Layton was entirely at the Dimsdales' mercy.

Why else would she remain in their employ when the children hurled abuse at her? When they bullied her? Struck her, by God? And now this insult to heap atop the rest. The very worst insult by Jack's reckoning.

Dimsdale's face relaxed into a too jovial smile. "There, you see? Nothing to trouble yourself over. Just having a word with one of my staff about a small domestic matter."

Jack didn't believe it for a second. "I think not," he said. "Not in your condition."

Dimsdale's smile wavered. "I say, Beresford. This is really none of your business."

Jack took a threatening step toward him. He may have a gammy leg, but he could still deal with a man of Dimsdale's ilk. "I'm making it my business," he said. "You're unfit for company. I suggest you retire to your cabin until you've sobered up."

Dimsdale scrunched his brow, as though he were attempting to solve a thorny mathematical problem. If he could exercise his feeble wit to the task, he'd realize that Jack was giving him an out. A means of blaming his despicable behavior on drink when they both knew it was a question, not of whiskey, but of character.

"Now you mention it, I did overindulge a bit at the gaming tables," Dimsdale replied at last. "Congenial company, and a rousing evening of cards. Not unheard of for a gentleman, but I take your meaning. A good night's rest will see me straight." Offering Jack a teetering bow, he backed away, but not before casting a flinty look in Miss Layton's direction. "You may address yourself to my wife in the morning," he said to her. "She will see to any arrangements."

With that, he staggered off in the direction of the stairs that led to the deck below.

No sooner had he gone than Miss Layton's shoulders slumped. A visible tremor went through her. She rested both of her hands on the rail of the ship to steady herself.

"Arrangements about what?" Jack asked.

Miss Layton's reply was little more than a whisper. "About my dismissal, I fear."

Jack was incredulous. "You believe you're going to be sacked?"

"Undoubtedly."

He came to stand beside her. "But why?"

"For upsetting the status quo."

Jack's temper rose. "For refusing his advances, you mean."

Miss Layton didn't look at him. "And for complaining about the children. And failing to manage them. And not being suitably deferential. And yes, for refusing his advances."

Jack muttered an oath.

Miss Layton flinched. "Must you use such coarse language?"

"If ever there was a time for it," he said.

She cut him a glance. Her eyes narrowed. "Are you *really* the son of the Earl of Allendale?"

"I am."

"Not the one who was very nearly engaged to Miss Faraday?"

Jack's mouth hitched briefly. "You've heard of me?"

Miss Layton didn't appear amused. Her porcelain blue gaze was all too incisive. "Is *that* why you're traveling incognito?"

"The chief reason," Jack admitted.

She huffed. There was no humor in the sound. "How novel."

"Is it?"

"To be some glorious creature all the young ladies are hunting?"

He cocked a brow at her. "Glorious?"

Her cheeks turned the exact color of the pale pink musk mallows that dotted the landscape near his childhood home in Somerset. "I only meant—"

"I know what you meant," he said. "What people like you don't readily consider is that the hunt is only ever enjoyable for the hunter, not the hunted. Particularly when we'd prefer not to be caught." He studied her face. She was worryingly pale behind her blush. "*Are* you all right?"

She managed a faint smile. "One hunted creature to another?"

"If you like."

"I suppose I *am* a trifle shaken," she said. "But I shall be well directly."

Jack gestured to a pair of deck chairs arranged beneath one of the hanging lamps. Miss Layton wordlessly preceded him there, taking a seat. Jack sat down in the chair across from her, glad to relieve the weight on his leg.

"What can I do?" he asked.

"Nothing," she replied. "No one can." The shadow of a smile vanished from her lips. It was replaced with a look of resignation. "If Mrs. Dimsdale sees fit to dismiss me in the morning, I shall have nothing, and nowhere to turn."

"Come now. We're nearly to England. It isn't as if she can toss you over the side and command you to swim the remainder of the way home."

"I wouldn't put it past her."

"In all seriousness—"

"In all seriousness," Miss Layton said, "swimming would be preferable to the alternative." She folded her hands tight in her lap. "She'll likely demand that I pay her back for my fare. That was the agreement, passage home from India in exchange for my looking after the four children."

"Was there anything in that agreement about physical abuse? Or about being subjected to overtures made by the family patriarch?"

"Of course not."

"Then—"

"You're speaking as though any of it were fair. As though their conduct to me was governed by law, or... or basic good manners. It isn't that way with servants. We're at the mercy of our employers. And if you're me..." She trailed off, shaking her head.

"Go on," Jack prompted.

She took a deep breath. "Being a governess is already difficult."

"Because of the Dimsdale children."

"No. That is . . . yes, but not only because of them. It's the position itself that poses the problem." She hesitated again before explaining, "A governess is neither lady, nor servant. We lead an in-between existence, snubbed by our betters and shunned by those who feel we think we're better than them. It's a fact in even the finest houses, and with the very best, most capable governesses. And I . . . I am *not* the best governess."

Jack's throat tightened. She looked so alone. So defeated. He had to stifle the urge to set a reassuring hand on her shoulder. It's what he would have done if she were his younger sister, Kate.

But the last thing Miss Layton needed right now was another man pawing at her, however well intended.

"You're too severe on yourself," he said.

"I am not," she informed him. And then: "Service hasn't come easily to me. I'm constantly failing. Making mistakes. I can't converse in fluent French. I regularly mistake countries on the globe. I'm over-opinionated, I laugh too much, and I too often speak my mind. If that doesn't convince you I'm a lost cause—"

"Not at all," Jack said stoutly. "It makes me like you all the more."

"You're just trying to reassure me."

"Precisely. A heroic effort too, if I say so myself. I would that you could do the same for me."

"You don't require my reassurance," she said, dashing the heel of her hand across her cheek.

Jack started. Good lord. Was she wiping away a tear?

She glanced at him again when he didn't answer. Her eyes were indeed damp. "Do you?" she asked.

"You seem to forget that I just told your employer who I am," Jack said.

"He's in no condition to repeat the information."

"Not tonight he isn't, but in the morning, he'll be broadcasting it all over the ship. First to his wife, then to his friends in the gaming saloon. From there, the news will spread like wildfire."

Jack could already imagine the result.

The instant Mrs. Farraday learned he was on board, she would be fast on his scent, keen as a hound at the commencement of foxhunting season. And Jack was no longer a healthy fox, capable of outrunning his pursuer. The odds were far greater than usual that he'd be cornered, trapped, caught.

Miss Layton's brow puckered. "Truly? But then—"

"The hunt for one Jack Beresford will resume," Jack pronounced grimly.

A spark of feminine interest flickered at the back of her gaze. "Is that your given name? Jack?"

"It is." He smiled, briefly diverted. "Dare I ask yours?"

"Beatrice," she said. "Or Bea, if you like. That's what my parents called me before they passed away."

Jack's fleeting smile was transformed into a wince. *Bloody hell.* On top of everything else, she was an orphan?

Miss Layton—or Bea—didn't seem to register his reaction. "May I ask you something personal?" she inquired. She didn't wait for his reply. "Why don't you wish to marry Miss Faraday?"

"I don't wish to marry anyone," he said.

She examined his face in the lamplight. "You object to the institution?"

"On the contrary," Jack said. "I think marriage a fine thing. My parents are deliriously happy in theirs. My siblings are too, or so they claim. They've all entered into love matches. It's the Beresford way, to marry for some grand passion. Makes one rather reluctant to settle for anything less."

"I didn't know gentlemen considered such things."

"I can't speak for all gentlemen," he said. "Only myself."

"And you don't believe you could feel such a passion for Miss Farraday? But why not? She's lovely to look at. *And* she's surprisingly kind. She helped me with Miss Dimsdale today when I was struggling with her. Few ladies would have done the same."

Jack was unmoved by recitations of Miss Farraday's finer qualities. "I don't care to be chased."

"And now you will be, thanks to me." Bea's expression took on another layer of anguish. She hung her head. "Oh, but this is all my fault!"

Jack raked a hand through his hair. "Aren't we a fine pair? Two desperate souls stuck on this blasted ship, at the mercy of everyone else." He exhaled a heavy sigh. "Our lives are going to look very different tomorrow if things develop in the way we expect."

"Yes, they will," Bea acknowledged bleakly.

"Perhaps we might revisit jumping overboard?" Jack suggested, only half in jest.

"*You* needn't do so. The worst that could happen to you is an entanglement with an exceptionally beautiful young lady. While I—" There was a pitiful catch in her voice. "I may not have forfeited my position, but I'm certain to have forfeited my reference. Who in England will ever hire me now? I'm as likely to starve in the street as to find respectable employment. The only hope I have is to throw myself on Mrs. Dimsdale's mercy. A slim hope at best, for she has no mercy that I've ever seen."

Jack regarded Bea in the shadows cast from the softly swaying lamp above. She was an orphan, with no friends and no family, soon to be sacked from the very position that was ensuring her passage home.

While he—

He could no longer walk unaided, let alone run. Until such time as he healed from his latest surgery, he was completely reliant on his cane. Without it, he'd be something worse than an injured fox. He'd be a sitting duck.

Unless...

An idea entered his head.

A *reckless* idea.

Jack's pulse leapt. It had been far too long since he'd had such a wild notion. He'd begun to fear he never would again. But there it was, as clear as day, firing his senses and burning in his blood.

And really, Jack told himself, the idea wasn't entirely foolhardy. When looked at in the right light, it was downright sensible.

"I think I may have struck on a solution," he said as it began to take shape in his mind.

Bea raised her head. "For you or for me?"

"For both of us," Jack said. "All it requires is that we engage in a very small act of subterfuge."

A doubtful frown darkened her gaze.

Jack plunged ahead. "Tell me," he said. "Would you be at all opposed to pretending that we're engaged?"

# Chapter Seven

Bea stared at him, stunned. "*That's* what you call 'a very small act of subterfuge?'"

"You must admit," Jack said. "It would do the trick."

"To pretend that we're engaged to be married?" Bea didn't know whether to laugh or to spring up from her seat and flee. The latter, she suspected, given the sheer absurdity of the suggestion. Whoever he was, Jack Beresford was clearly insane.

"Just until we reach England," he said as if it were the most sensible thing in the world.

She moved to stand. "Forgive me. I'm rather overset. I expect you are too else you'd never have suggested—"

Jack caught hold of her hand. "Wait."

Bea froze as his fingers engulfed hers. His skin was warm, his grip strong and reassuring. Her heart skipped a beat as he tugged her back downward. She reluctantly resumed her seat.

Jack didn't release her hand. "Forget how ridiculous it

sounds on its face," he said. "It's the logic of it that's important."

"I dispute the logic," Bea said. "The mere suggestion is patently absurd, as well as being offensive. If I didn't know better, I'd think you were making sport of—"

"Listen to me," Jack said. "If I was your fiancé, *I* would be responsible for you, not the Dimsdales. I could see that you were comfortable. Looked after. And more importantly, safe. And if you were mine..."

Butterflies fluttered to life in Bea's stomach. An uneasy sensation, and one she was entirely unaccustomed to. For the second time that night, she felt clammy and breathless.

"I would be off the market," he continued. "As good as taken. There would be no more point in anyone or their mother chasing me."

Bea reluctantly slipped her hand from his. As delicious as the press of his fingers felt on hers, this wasn't a conversation for butterflies and breathlessness. What this discussion required was cold common sense.

"You're willfully oversimplifying the matter," she said. "And you're forgetting that ladies can be ruthless. If they want you enough, they'll find a way. My existence won't stop them. Not when I am who I am—a governess with no family or connection. No truly determined female would think anything of supplanting me."

"No one would supplant you," Jack vowed.

The butterflies batted their wings again. Bea did her best to ignore them. "You mistake my point."

"Which is?"

"That you could still be trapped regardless," she said. "Don't you see? What's to stop Mrs. Farraday from conspiring to get you alone with her daughter? Or for anyone else on board to do the same?"

"Because *you'll* be with me," Jack replied. "In my company, all the time, from the moment I emerge from my cabin in the morning, until I retire at night."

"*All* the time?" Bea echoed. "It would never be permitted."

"It would," he assured her. "If we were engaged, no one could object."

Bea clasped her hands in her lap. She didn't want to think of what being engaged to Jack Beresford might be like. Even if it *was* only pretend.

"And how do you know *I* won't trap you, once I have you in my clutches?" she asked.

Jack went peculiarly still.

Her lips thinned in a somber smile. So, he hadn't thought of everything. It was unsurprising. All the same...

She'd have preferred he didn't look so horrified at the prospect of finding himself shackled to her in earnest.

"I could, you know," she said. "Once the engagement has been announced, you'll find it difficult to break things off without my cooperation."

"You wouldn't—"

"Of course not," she said scornfully. As if she was so desperate as to trap a gentleman into marriage! "But you have no way of knowing that, do you? There are no guarantees aside from my word."

"I could do the same to you," Jack pointed out. "Announce the engagement and then insist that you go through with it."

She huffed a bitter laugh. "I very much doubt that you—"

"But you take my meaning. For this to work, we would have to trust each other."

"*Trust* each other? We scarcely *know* each other!"

"Nonsense. We've had several meaningful conversations in the moonlight. One brush with danger, courtesy of your employer. One heroic moment, courtesy of me. And now we've made common cause."

"I hardly think—"

"Most couples speak for three minutes at the edge of a ballroom and consider themselves very well acquainted indeed, but you and I—"

"*Must* you refer to us as a couple?"

"A make-believe couple," he amended.

"Who met... where?" she asked in increasing disbelief. "What conceivable lie could we hope to formulate about how this engagement came to pass?"

"We'd tell the truth," Jack said. "That we met on this ship, in the moonlight. We'll say you stole my heart away under the stars. Or vice versa. Who would dare to argue?"

His offhand words were possessed of an insidious power. They settled somewhere in Bea's heart, warm and deep. A romance in the moonlight, under the stars. A product, perhaps, of all those futile wishes she'd made. Wishes for a better life. A purpose. Something—anything—that would bring her true happiness.

What if this was the answer to those wishes?

But no.

*No.*

This wasn't real. This was a deranged jest.

Bea shook her head. "It defies common sense."

"On the contrary," Jack said. "It's logical, as I told you. The only option, really."

Her gaze returned to his. His ice-gray eyes were blazing with certainty.

Her heart gave another mutinous double thump.

Good heavens. He *must* be out of his wits. It happened sometimes, didn't it, with soldiers returning from the wars? Was one supposed to reason with them? Or was it better to humor them?

Bea was at a complete loss.

She swallowed hard. "And if I did agree to this ridiculous scheme... What would happen when we arrive in England?"

"We'd have an amicable parting," Jack said.

"A broken engagement?"

"By mutual decision, with no acrimony. We would go our separate ways at Southampton with our reputations intact."

Bea pressed her fingers to her temple. She feared she was losing her mind too. She must be, for Jack's outrageous plan was starting to sound like a rather appealing remedy to her problem.

But not *all* of her problems.

"You forget," she said. "I'll have lost my reference. Without one—"

"I can get you a reference," Jack said with unerring confidence. "A position too, if it comes to it."

She snorted in disbelief.

"I mean it," he said. "Do you know how many children my brothers and sister have between them? And those children have friends. Somewhere among them there must be one in need of a governess."

Bea's hand fell from her brow. She was suddenly unbelievably weary. "It appears you have an answer for every difficulty."

"Because there is one," he said. "That's how perfect of a solution this would be."

She forced herself to meet his eyes. Speaking of perfect...

"You're forgetting the most important thing," she said.

"I don't think so. We've covered my safety and yours, arrangements for the remainder of the voyage, our amicable breakup, and my finding you respectable employment. As to money, you need have no concern on that score. I'm comfortably enough off to reimburse the Dimsdales for your passage and anything else they—"

"It isn't money," Bea said. "It's Hannah."

---

JACK BLINKED. *"WHAT?"*

"Hannah," she enunciated as though he hadn't heard her properly. "The lady who wrote the letter you're constantly rereading."

Jack stared at her in dawning understanding. "Ah." His mouth tipped at one corner. "*That* Hannah."

"Quite," Bea said briskly. "I don't know about *her*, but if *I* were your sweetheart, I wouldn't appreciate you pretending to be engaged to some ramshackle stranger you'd met on a sea voyage."

"You'll find that Hannah is quite understanding."

"Not about this, surely."

"Even about this," Jack said. "And even after being married to my oldest brother for the past fourteen years. James has no sense of humor himself. I'm amazed he hasn't rubbed off on her."

Bea's jaw went slack. "Do you mean to say that Hannah is your—"

"My sister-in-law," Jack said. "Hannah Beresford, Viscountess St. Clare. She's a capital correspondent."

Bea collected herself with admirable swiftness, but not before Jack spied a glint of relief in her face.

It heartened him.

The fact that she was relieved to discover that he was free of entanglements meant she was considering his proposal.

Or rather, his *plan*.

Because it wasn't an actual proposal. Heaven forbid. Jack had never proposed to a girl in his life. And he didn't intend to start now, with a little sparrow of a starchy governess. No matter *how* fine her eyes.

"We're actually related twice over," he continued as casually as if they were discussing the weather. "My little sister, Kate, is married to Hannah's older brother, Charles Heywood. As for myself—" He smiled again. "I have no sweetheart."

"Don't you?"

"Not that I'm aware of. I'm a lone wolf, me. Always have been. So, you see... There's nothing on that score that would prevent us from moving forward with our plan."

"*Your* plan," Bea said. "I'm far too old for such a childish prank."

"I'm not," Jack said frankly. "Not if it serves."

"And you truly believe it will?"

"I do. Indeed, I'm rather impressed at the way it all comes together. Nothing will be left to chance. Nothing can go wrong."

"Famous last words," Bea muttered. She abruptly stood. "I'm afraid my answer is no."

Jack was at once on his feet. He felt an inexplicable surge of panic. "Don't say that."

"You'll be grateful I did in the morning. The whole idea is madness. The mere suggestion of it would send the entire ship into a frenzy."

"I don't care about anyone else on the ship," Jack said with brutal candor. "I care about *us*."

Bea's rigid face betrayed a raw flash of longing. It softened her eyes and her mouth, making her appear, for an instant, far younger, and far more uncertain, than she was.

She marshaled herself directly. But once seen, it couldn't be unseen.

*This* is what existed beneath that hard exterior. A woman of profound loveliness and vulnerability, with a tender gaze and alarmingly kissable lips.

Jack stared at her, feeling oddly off balance. "Beatrice," he said. "Bea. I—"

She cut him off before he could finish. "Goodnight, Mr. Beresford. I thank you again for the assistance you rendered me." She turned to walk past him, the swell of her skirts brushing against his leg.

Jack caught her arm. His voice deepened. "At least say you'll think about it."

Bea bent her head. For a long moment, there was only the sound of her breath and his, and that of the crashing sea around them. "Very well," she said finally. "Only let me go. Please."

Jack promptly released her. Gripping his cane as she moved to leave, he offered her a bow. By the time he straightened, she was gone.

# Chapter Eight

"Mr. Dimsdale said *that?*" Pearl was aghast. "And it was Mr. Beresford who—"

"*Colonel* Beresford." Dousing the lantern, Bea crawled into her berth. Her heavy cotton nightgown and thick wool socks did nothing to dispel the lingering gooseflesh on her skin. She was chilled to the bone. She must be. Why else was she still trembling? "And yes, on both counts."

Pearl climbed down from her upper berth in the darkness, landing on the gently rocking floor of the ship with a soft thud. She relit the lantern. Half-asleep when Bea had entered the cabin, she was now wide-eyed and alert. "You can't leave it at that!"

Bea sat back against the wall, curling her legs beneath her. "What else is there to say?"

Pearl fetched a shawl. She drew it around her nightgown-clad figure before joining Bea in the lower berth. "Are you *sure* he said his name was Beresford?"

"Of course, I am."

"The son of the Earl of Allendale?"

"That's what he claimed."

Pearl shook her head, unable to believe it. "And on this ship the whole time? If he's telling the truth—"

"I don't know why he wouldn't be," Bea said.

Even as she uttered the words, a small voice at the back of her head reminded her of what had *really* transpired this evening.

As if Bea could ever forget!

Jack hadn't just rescued her. He'd *proposed* to her. And not a real proposal, either. Bea had never been so fortunate as to receive one of those. Instead, he'd had the temerity to suggest that the two of them pretend to be engaged to each other.

It was a scandalous notion, and one that revealed, more than anything, Jack Beresford's cavalier attitude toward the truth.

Pearl would certainly be fascinated to hear of it. But Bea had no intention of sharing the story. Jack's proposition had been too shocking. Too...

Oh, Bea hated to admit it to herself, but it was too ridiculously precious. Just the sort of vaguely romantic secret an old maid might keep under her pillow during all the lonely years of her life.

A depressing thought.

"Was he outrageously handsome?" Pearl asked.

Heat crept up Bea's throat. She prayed Pearl wouldn't notice it. "Not outrageously," she said. "But... Yes. He *is* handsome."

Pearl snuggled beside her. "Colonel Beresford was *outrageously* handsome," she said. "I saw him once in Delhi. It was when he first met the Farradays. He was in company with some General Sahib, surveying the troops. He stayed for over a fortnight. All the ladies were beside themselves. There were dances and dinners, and a flurry of new gowns made with the finest silks and lace. Mrs. Rawson was often called upon to provide introductions."

"Mrs. Rawson is acquainted with Colonel Beresford?"

"No, but she met his oldest brother once, many years ago, at an assembly in Bath. She still talks about it."

"I've never heard her."

"You never hear anything. You're forever off with the children. But I remain with the ladies. I hear *everything*."

Bea hated that she was curious. "Is there so much to hear?"

"Oh yes." Pearl drew the coarse blanket up over them in the berth. "According to Mrs. Rawson, Colonel Beresford fought in the Crimea before coming to Delhi. But India didn't sit well with him. He left shortly after for Persia, and from there to Egypt on extended leave. Mrs. Farraday found out he would be staying at Shepheard's Hotel, and arranged that she and her daughter would be there too. *That* was when she nearly caught him."

Bea felt a sharp twinge of pity for Jack. Goodness. He really *had* been pursued. "Fortunately for him, he managed to get away," she observed dryly.

"It wasn't the first time he'd been chased, I don't wonder," Pearl said. "He returned to fighting in Persia before Mrs. Farraday could play her final card. When she heard he was badly injured in some battle in the desert, she feared he'd been killed and that she'd lost her chance forever."

"But he didn't die," Bea pointed out. "Obviously."

He'd said that his horse had fallen on him, and that he'd

had several surgeries to repair the damage. That admission too had been exceedingly cavalier. Still...

Bea had sensed there was something more behind it. Regret, bitterness, possibly even anger.

"Which was splendid news for Mrs. Farraday and her daughter," Pearl went on. "Once she learned that he'd survived, and that he'd returned to Cairo for surgery, she made inquiries at all the local hospitals, but was unable to find him. Mrs. Rawson claims that Mrs. Farraday would be there still, searching the four corners of the city, if her money hadn't begun to run out."

Bea swallowed the acrid taste in her mouth. Jack Beresford was more than capable of taking care of himself. Even so, she hated to think of him lying injured in a hospital bed, barely conscious after surgery, a helpless victim to any scheming, marriage-minded mama who was determined to capture him.

"I hadn't realized Mrs. Farraday was so ruthless in her efforts," she said.

"Any mother might be," Pearl replied. "Colonel Beresford is a prize."

"Nonsense. He's no trophy for Mrs. Farraday to hang on her wall."

"No, indeed. She intends to hang him on her daughter's wall."

"Really, Pearl," Bea chided.

Pearl giggled. "When she discovers that he's on the ship—"

Bea shot her a sharp look. "You mustn't say a word."

"They wouldn't listen if I did," Pearl said. "To them, I'm invisible."

Bea was immediately chastened. Her problems were

nothing in comparison to the trials Pearl must have endured as a servant of mixed heritage. "I'm sorry," she said.

"I'm not." Pearl's smile turned impish. "Invisibility has its benefits. You would do well to cultivate it if you mean to remain in your position."

Bea feared that ship had already sailed. "It's too late for invisibility where I'm concerned," she said. "Whatever happens to me tomorrow, I have a sinking feeling that everyone on this ship is going to hear about it."

"THE DAY YOU'VE LONG BEEN AWAITING HAS finally arrived, Maberly," Jack said on rising the next morning. He passed his batman the shaving razor. "Shear me."

Maberly accepted the implement with a look of skepticism. "Are you in earnest, sir?"

"I've never been more so." Jack sat down in the wooden chair near the washstand in his cabin, his injured leg stretched out before him. If he once again had to be Jack Beresford, he intended to be him in every way. And Jack Beresford never sported a beard or mustache.

Maberly got straight to work lathering the shaving soap. "And your hair?"

"Trim it," Jack said. "As of today, you and I will be joining the rest of the passengers."

Maberly stilled. "What about Mrs. Farraday and the other ladies?"

"It will doubtless be unpleasant," Jack allowed. "But it's out of my hands now."

Maberly looked at him in question.

"I revealed my identity to someone above deck last night," Jack said.

The batman's eyes darkened with disapproval. "Not that sad governess who works for those loud colonials?"

"No." Jack frowned. "And she's not a 'sad governess.' She's rather resilient, in fact. A survivor." He leaned back in the chair as Maberly stropped the razor. "Did you know she's had over two dozen postings?"

"Is that meant to be impressive?"

"She's been in India less than a decade. It equals out to nearly three postings per year."

"So," Maberly mused. "She can't keep a job."

"It seems not. Which goes a long way to explaining how she ended up working for the Dimsdale family." Jack's frown deepened. "It was he who I revealed myself to last night. The Dimsdale fellow."

Maberly lathered Jack's jaw. "Unwise, I'd have thought."

"But necessary."

"If you say so, sir." Maberly began to shave him. "Don't change the fact that it will set those Farraday women to chasing you again. And if I may point out—"

"As if I could stop you."

"—you ain't as fleet of foot as you once was."

Jack closed his eyes. "No. I'm not. But I *am* happy to be leaving this cabin, whatever the outcome."

"Still, it ain't going to be easy going for the rest of the voyage."

"No," Jack acknowledged grimly.

Relieved as he was to shed the confines of his self-imposed exile, he didn't much look forward to the social interaction that would inevitably come with it. He'd have to be on his guard at all moments, wary of every trap and snare.

It promised to be an exhausting business. Possibly a futile one too, given the determination of Mrs. Farraday.

As Maberly scraped the beard from Jack's face and throat, Jack brooded over how much easier it all might have been if only Bea had been willing to tell the others that they were engaged.

Granted, she *had* agreed to think about it, but even if she did, Jack held out little hope that she'd change her mind. She was too sensible, that was the trouble. Too cautious.

Too scared.

It was that which troubled him. Knowing that she was frightened of being sacked, and left without a reference. That, absent his support, she'd be forced to face the consequences of Mr. Dimsdale's actions alone.

And what could Jack do about it? Nothing at all. Not without a formal claim on her. And he couldn't very well force her to pretend that he was her fiancé, could he?

Perhaps it had been a foolish idea anyway. Especially given the unsettling flashes of attraction Jack had lately been feeling for her.

A short time later, he emerged from his cabin, clad in a well-cut black coat and gray flannel trousers, his face clean-shaven and his hair combed into meticulous order. Breakfast was already being served in the dining saloon. To get there, Jack had to pass through the grand saloon on the main deck.

He heard the shrilly raised voice of a woman well before he arrived there.

"—unable to manage the slightest thing, and forever complaining to me, and now to my husband!" The harsh words rang down the hall. "Oh yes, he informed me of your disrespect. I daresay you thought it would go unpunished, dependent as we are on you to look after the children."

"*My* disrespect?" Bea's voice echoed. "It was *your* husband who behaved disrespectfully, ma'am. He was well in his cups, and made overtures to me of an inappropriate nature."

Jack flinched at the brutality of Bea's unapologetic honesty. Good lord, so much for throwing herself on her employer's mercy! Somewhere between the anguished tears she'd shed last night, and facing Mrs. Dimsdale this morning, Bea must have decided it was as well to be hanged for a sheep as a lamb.

"How *dare* you!" Mrs. Dimsdale cried.

"As for my complaining," Bea continued sharply, "I wouldn't have to if your children were possessed of a shred of basic good manners."

"Insolent jade! I won't hear another word—"

"There's a reason you've been unable to keep a governess for them. And it's got nothing to do with those governess's failings, and everything to do with your failures as a parent."

"Hateful creature!" Mrs. Dimsdale's reply vibrated with fury. "First you malign my husband, and now my sons and my innocent daughter? Be grateful I'm only dismissing you. I could just as easily have you arrested for fraud and for obtaining this position by false pretenses!"

Jack's blood ran cold. Could she, by heaven? He would see about that.

Tightening his hand on his cane, he limped into the saloon. Bea stood at attention in front of an expensively clad, red-faced lady seated in a tall-backed chair. Mrs. Dimsdale, Jack presumed. Her chin was wobbling with fury.

"For that's what you did, I vow," she went on scathingly. "Accepted employment with us purely to secure your passage. You had no intention of doing the work for which we hired you. And you shan't do it now. I'll have no devious slatterns in my household. As to the monies you owe us for your board and fare—"

"Good morning, ladies," Jack said suavely.

Bea's head turned with a start. Her blue eyes widened, taking in the whole of him—from the close-cropped layers of his golden-blond hair to the polished sheen of his boots—in one arrested glance.

Mrs. Dimsdale did the same, yet nowhere near as discreetly. Her eyes bulged and her mouth fell open. She stared at Jack for a full five seconds before closing it. "I declare—it can't be, can it?" She moved to stand. "Upon my soul, but it *is!* Colonel Beresford, a passenger on the Pera! Why did no one tell me of this?"

"You have the advantage of me, ma'am," Jack said. "You know my name, yet I have no recollection of meeting you."

Mrs. Dimsdale hurried to greet him, the lace trimming on her morning gown rustling loudly in the sudden silence of the saloon. "We were never formally introduced. But I was in Delhi when you visited with General Havelock." Stopping in front of Jack, she dropped him a deep curtsy. "You might remember my husband, Mr. Dimsdale. He often played polo with the officers."

"In fact, I met your husband last night," Jack said. "An encounter I'm not likely to forget."

Mrs. Dimsdale's smile wavered at the lack of warmth in Jack's words. She shot a look at Bea, as though she were to blame for it.

Bea remained standing by the chair. She was wearing one of her plain wool dresses again, but there was nothing else plain about her. Not today. Rather than looking cowed or fearful, she appeared as formidable as a diminutive

Amazon, with bright eyes and cheeks flushed, not with blushes this time, but with something approaching anger.

Jack's heart performed a disconcerting somersault.

"I must apologize," Mrs. Dimsdale said to him. "You've caught me in the middle of a minor domestic matter. *That* person is a former servant of mine who I've been given cause to discharge."

"Can I be of assistance?" Jack inquired.

"How very gallant of you to offer," Mrs. Dimsdale replied with a girlish titter. "I would be—"

"I wasn't asking you, ma'am," Jack said. "I was asking Miss Layton."

# Chapter Nine

It was all Bea could do not to gawp at Jack like a beached mackerel.

So, *this* is what all the fuss was over. The reason he had been hounded across continents, pursued like some mythical golden hind.

He wasn't only handsome.

He was, as Pearl had stated, *outrageously* handsome.

Far too handsome to be troubling himself over Bea's problems. And yet, he was doing just that.

Her chest tightened on an unnerving swell of gratitude.

Until this moment, she had been resigned to forging ahead on her own. And doing a rather good job of it, she thought, despite the certain knowledge that she was burning her bridges behind her. But to have Jack appear in all his splendor, and for him to ally himself with her, was akin to having a crushing weight lifted from her shoulders.

For the first time in Bea's life, she wasn't facing the firing squad alone.

Mrs. Dimsdale's thin brows elevated all the way to her

hairline. "Do you mean to say that you know my children's governess, Colonel Beresford?"

"I have that honor," Jack replied.

Mrs. Dimsdale looked between the two of them with swift displeasure. There was only one reason an impoverished governess would be acquainted with an unmarried gentleman who was not of her class and it had nothing to do with honor.

"So," she said, turning on Bea. "Your crimes have managed to outpace even the ones for which you stand accused. Not content with defiance and deception, you've seen fit to add harlotry to your list."

Bea's cheeks burned with mortification. In all her many trips before various firing squads over the years, she'd never yet been accused of *that*. Impertinence, yes. Even insubordination. But never a lapse of morality.

Jack's expression was transformed by a thunderous scowl. "Now see here, madam—"

"You misunderstand," Bea said at the same time. "Colonel Beresford and I are—"

"Are what?" Mrs. Dimsdale demanded.

Bea's gaze found Jack's. They're eyes met for a weighted moment. Something seemed to pass between them. Bea felt it as surely as if he'd taken her hand just as he had last night, his voice deep and his manner reassuring, promising her that his plan "would solve everything."

This time, Bea believed it.

The words emerged from her lips before she could stop them. "We are engaged to be married."

Mrs. Dimsdale's face drained of color. "You're *what?*"

"Miss Layton and I are engaged," Jack confirmed without missing a beat.

The next thing Bea knew, he was at her side. She had no memory of him walking there, or of anything else for that matter. She feared she may have fallen into some manner of self-induced shock.

"Naturally she can no longer remain in your employ," Jack said. "She's under my protection now. As to the accusations you've levied—" He took a step toward Mrs. Dimsdale, sufficient to make her draw back. "I'll thank you not to repeat them. You will find me woefully absent a sense of humor when it comes to gossip about the lady who is soon-to-be my wife."

"But Colonel," Mrs. Dimsdale sputtered. "How can you—How can *she*—It isn't at all—"

"If you have any other issues, you may bring them to me," Jack said. "Miss Layton is not to be bothered by you. *Or* by your husband."

Mrs. Dimsdale blanched. "I don't know what you're implying, but—"

"Now, if you will excuse us?" Jack offered Bea his arm. "Shall we go into breakfast, my dear?"

Bea took it numbly. *My dear*, he'd called her. She moistened her lips. Her mouth was suddenly dry. "I'm sorry," she said. "I seem to have lost my appetite."

Jack didn't bat an eye. "A breath of fresh air, then."

Bea nodded. She held tight to Jack's arm as he led her from the saloon, leaving Mrs. Dimsdale behind them.

And *what have I done?* Bea thought.

*Good lord above, what on earth have I done?*

Jack withdrew a small silver flask from the interior pocket of his coat. He unscrewed the cap before passing it to Bea. She was at the rail of the ship, her face to the sea. The breeze over the water played in the loose tendrils of dark hair that framed her pale countenance.

"Here," he said. "Have a swig of this."

She did as he bid her, grimacing mightily at the taste of it. "What was *that?*"

"Whiskey," he said. "For shock."

She thrust the flask back at him in disgust. "I'm not *in* shock."

Jack made no reply as he screwed the cap back on. During his many years in the army, he'd become a keen observer of men. He knew when they were lying to him, when they were foxed, and when they were frightened. And he knew when one of them had succumbed to shock.

It was the latter that had come over Bea. Jack had seen it happen the instant she'd announced that the two of them were engaged. Her face had gone waxen, and her gaze had become fixed. He'd been amazed she hadn't swooned.

She set her hands on the rail. "I didn't expect that you—" she broke off. "That is, I didn't consider what must come next."

"Which part?" Jack asked. They'd discussed all of it last night, hadn't they? He believed he'd been thorough. He usually was, even with the most reckless of his brainstorms.

"What you said about my being under your protection," she replied.

"We talked about that, didn't we?" Jack returned his flask to his pocket. "Not that you require my protection. You seemed to be doing an excellent job of protecting yourself when I entered the saloon." He smiled slightly. "What happened to throwing yourself on Mrs. Dimsdale's mercy?"

Bea gave an eloquent grimace. "My wretched temper."

Jack's smile broadened with reluctant amusement. He leaned against the rail at her side. "I wasn't aware you had one."

"Didn't I mention it last night when I was giving you a catalog of my failings?"

"Not that I recall."

She'd enumerated countless flaws. Claimed she was bold, difficult, opinionated. Even that she was bad at geography. But she hadn't said anything about having a temper.

"It creeps up on me," she explained morosely. "The smallest offenses accruing day-by-day until I can bear it no longer without speaking up. That's what happened with Mrs. Dimsdale. I was standing in front of her, fully prepared to beg her pardon for all my supposed crimes, when the injustice of the situation became too great to ignore."

"It would indeed have been an injustice had she sacked you for her husband's offense," Jack said.

"Exactly what I thought," Bea said. "But being in the right is poor comfort, given what's happened as a result. This situation—you and I—It's... It's an absolute catastrophe."

Jack had never imagined that a woman—*any* woman—would describe being engaged to him as a catastrophe. Even if it *was* only a fake engagement. The fact that Bea had done so, and that she continued to look so glum, was equal parts amusing and insulting.

"Mrs. Dimsdale is probably telling everyone as we speak," she said. "Her husband, Mrs. Rawson, the Farradays, the children. The captain and the crew. The stewards and the—"

"Very likely."

"I can't imagine what they must be saying about me."

"Who cares?" Jack asked. "It can't touch you now."

Bea's fingers curled tighter on the rail. She stared out at the sea. "Poor Pearl."

He frowned. "Who is Pearl?"

"Mrs. Rawson's maid-companion. We've shared quarters since we left Bombay. She's become my friend. And now... She must hate me."

Jack feared he had lost the thread. "Why must she?"

Bea cast him a bleak glance. "It was she who Mrs. Dimsdale called upon to watch the children this morning. Mrs. Rawson must have lent her for the purpose. Otherwise, Mrs. Dimsdale wouldn't have been so quick to dismiss me."

"Ah." Jack began to understand. "Poor Pearl, indeed."

"So, you see," Bea said, releasing the rail, "we haven't considered everything."

"We didn't consider Pearl," Jack allowed. He racked his brain as Bea paced away from him. It didn't take him long to land upon a solution. "There's a simple enough remedy for it."

Bea didn't stop. She didn't appear to be listening, either. Arms folded, she walked toward the deck chairs beneath the awning.

Jack gripped his cane, following after her. "You'll require a maid for the remainder of the voyage. If Mrs. Rawson can lend Pearl to the Dimsdales, she can just as easily hire her out to you instead."

That got Bea's attention.

She stopped in her tracks, turning to face him. "Are you out of your senses? Pearl can't be my maid!"

"Why in blazes not?"

"She's my friend!"

Jack cocked a brow. "Ah," he said. "You have principles."

"And you don't?"

"Naturally I do. But if we're going to pull this off, we'll have to set them aside until we reach Southampton. In the meanwhile, all that matters is maintaining the fiction."

"By hiring Pearl to wait on me like a servant?" Bea looked appalled.

"You'll need a maid once you move into your stateroom. Better one that you're on good terms with than another gossiping stranger."

Bea stared at him. "*My stateroom?* You don't mean that—"

"You can't remain in servants' accommodation. Not when you're a Beresford bride to be."

Her jaw stiffened. "I'm not—"

"You *are*, as far as anyone else knows," Jack said, with a trace of impatience. "That's the whole point of this exercise. Which means that you must be treated as a lady, not as a governess, a washerwoman, or whatever else you've been accustomed to being."

"I have been whatever I've had to be to survive," she informed him stonily. "Governess, laundress, maid of all work. And now, apparently, your fake fiancée."

By her tone, one might easily be persuaded that all the positions were similarly distasteful.

"Quite," Jack said. "Which brings us to another matter."

It was something else he hadn't considered until this

moment. But Bea didn't need to know that. He'd rather she believed that he had all the elements of the plan well in hand than that he was making things up as he went along.

"What other matter?" she asked.

"When we arrive in Southampton, you'll have to take rooms at a hotel. You'll need somewhere to stay until I can arrange a position for you."

Judging by the grim look that came into Bea's eyes, she hadn't thought of this part of their plan either. "A hotel," she repeated flatly. "For how long?"

"A day or two at most. Just long enough for me to speak with my sister-in-law. I shall tell her—"

"That we're pretending to be engaged?"

"Lord no," Jack said, appalled.

He couldn't confide in Hannah about something like this. If he did, she'd inevitably tell James. And James was the last person on earth who could hear of it. He was too cold and implacable, lacking any trace of humor when it came to hare-brained schemes or breaches of gentlemanly conduct. If he learned that Jack had participated in such a deception, Jack would never hear the end of it.

"Then what?" Bea asked.

"I'll tell her the truth," Jack said. "That you're a hardworking, honorable, colonial governess, alone in the world, and anxious to find a position in a respectable British household."

"How succinctly you put it," Bea remarked dryly.

"Persuasively, I'd have said," Jack replied. "Hannah's got a good heart. She'll write you a reference straightaway."

"And I'm to rely on that possibility, am I? As I await this promised reference, alone in a strange hotel, with only a few shillings to my name?"

"You can rely on *me*."

"So you claim. But—"

"If this is to work—"

"Oh, what's the point?" Bea exclaimed in a burst of feeling. "I don't know what possessed me to tell Mrs. Dimsdale that you and I are engaged. She didn't believe it. The other passengers aren't going to believe it either."

"Not if you continue looking so dashed mournful, they won't," Jack snapped back, nettled. "If we were really engaged, you'd be smiling from ear to ear!"

Bea's eyes widened. She was startled into a choked laugh. "My goodness. You *do* think a lot of yourself."

Jack pushed his hand through his hair. The devil! He rarely permitted himself to be goaded into incivility. And he never boasted. Not to ladies, at any rate. And certainly not about himself.

At length, he managed a sheepish grimace. "Vanity, thy name is Beresford," he muttered. "If it makes any difference, I'm the least conceited of all my brothers."

"And the most pursued, I gather."

"Not by any conceivable measure. That distinction belongs to my oldest brother, James. Next to him and my second oldest brother, Ivo, my charms are decidedly third rate."

"I can scarcely credit *that*," she said.

Jack's mouth twitched. "If I didn't know you better, Miss Layton, I'd suspect that was a compliment."

"You don't know me at all, Colonel Beresford," she returned in repressive tones.

Her starchiness only made Jack's smile broaden. He was about to say something more when the unmistakable clatter of footsteps sounded from the stairs that led up from the deck below.

It seemed that Mrs. Dimsdale had wasted no time in informing the others of Jack's presence on board—*and* of his scandalous engagement to her disgraced former governess.

All that remained now was to face them.

"That will be the welcoming party," Jack said.

Bea's gaze jolted toward the stairs where the tall plumes on a pair of fashionable ladies' bonnets were just coming into view. The starch left her spine. Her face went a shade paler. "*Jack*—"

"All will be well," he assured her. "Granted, it's going to be bloody awkward, but once the formalities are out of the way—"

"I don't know if I can—"

"You can." He abruptly took her hand, enfolding it in his.

Bea's cheeks flushed pink, just as they had last night. But unlike last night, this time, she didn't pull away from him. Instead, she curled her ice-cold fingers around his in return, holding his hand tight.

Jack felt a disconcerting swell of protectiveness for her.

And that wasn't all.

There was something else there too. Some alarming quiver of heat that spiked his blood and made his heart lose its rhythm.

"I can't think how I'm to behave," she whispered as the other passengers began to appear.

"That's easy enough," he whispered back. "Just smile, Bea. And pretend you're wildly in love with me."

# Chapter Ten

Bea didn't know whether to laugh or to weep at Jack's wry directive. She'd never been in love with anyone, let alone *wildly* in love. How on earth was she to pretend to such a condition?

Naturally, there had been gentlemen she'd liked before. One couldn't reach the exalted age of nearly seven and twenty years without having encountered one or two of them. Though none stood out particularly in her memory. And certainly, none had inspired anything like butterflies.

They were all vague, faceless figures from days long gone by. The handsome young sailor who had shouldered her trunk for her at the docks when she'd first arrived in India as a girl of seventeen. The officer who had danced with her at the garden pavilion in Delhi. Or the bespectacled shopkeeper who had been so kind to her when she was struggling with her young charges during a trip to the bazaar in Calcutta.

*What about him?* she'd often thought during such fleeting encounters. *Could he be the one?*

Yet none of them ever had been. And soon—alarmingly soon—the day-to-day struggles of simply getting by had supplanted any fleeting romantic dreams of girlhood. Time had weighed against her, as had circumstance, leaving her older, harder, vastly more cynical.

During the last several years, had Jack crossed her path, Bea doubted whether she'd even have noticed him. But now that she had...

No, she supposed, it wouldn't be difficult to pretend.

Regrettably, there was no time to perfect her performance. The other passengers were already bearing down upon them. Among them were Mrs. Dimsdale, Mrs. Rawson, and Mrs. Farraday and her daughter.

They advanced on Jack and Bea with all the resoluteness of an invading army.

Bea's stomach trembled so she feared she might faint. Indeed, if not for the strength of Jack's hand holding hers, she very well might have done.

Gathering her courage, she forced herself to smile. Doubtless it looked more like a rictus of pain.

"Colonel Beresford! Upon my word!" Mrs. Farraday came ahead of the others, wearing an expression of forced cordiality. She curtsied in greeting. "What a sly trickster you are, sir. Mrs. Dimsdale informs us that you have been a passenger on the Pera this entire time!"

Jack inclined his head to her. "Mrs. Farraday. And Miss Farraday," he added as the younger lady joined her mother. "Always a pleasure."

Miss Farraday curtsied in turn. She was dressed all in pale yellow, a color that complemented her fair skin and dark hair to an exceptional degree. "Colonel Beresford."

Bea counseled herself not to be jealous. Miss Farraday

wasn't her enemy, simply because she was younger, lovelier, and more prettily dressed. All the same...

What woman wouldn't feel the burden of her own failings in the face of such unmarked perfection? Mere proximity made Bea conscious of every one of hers—the plainness of her features, the coarseness of her gown, and the redness of her ungloved hands.

"When did you board?" Mrs. Farraday demanded. "In Alexandria, I gather. Though I didn't see you on the docks. And I was keeping particular watch, so that I might be of assistance in your time of need."

Mrs. Dimsdale and Mrs. Rawson joined them before Jack could reply. The former examined Bea down the length of her nose before turning her attention to Jack. "Colonel Beresford," she said rigidly.

"Ma'am."

"You have met Mrs. Rawson?" Mrs. Dimsdale inquired, gesturing to the portly woman.

"We were introduced in Delhi," Mrs. Rawson reminded Jack as she tucked her little white Maltese dog, Benjamin, more securely under her arm. "It was when you visited camp with General Havelock. You may recall I'm acquainted with your brother, Viscount St. Clare."

"Of course." Jack acknowledged the lady with a bow. "I presume you've all met my fiancée, Miss Layton?"

Mrs. Rawson spared not a glance for Bea. "Then it's true? You *are* engaged?" she asked. "You have shocked us twice in one day, sir!"

"I told Mrs. Rawson that it must be one of your larks," Mrs. Farraday interjected. Like Mrs. Rawson, she pointedly avoided looking at Bea. "What else can it be? For I am informed that Mrs. Dimsdale's servant has been employed by her since leaving India. If you were in Cairo, how could the two of you have met—"

"I was in Cairo, ma'am," Jack said. "Recovering from another surgery. Since boarding the Pera, Miss Layton has been my only comfort."

Mrs. Farraday's mouth sagged. "But that was but six days ago!"

"Indeed, ma'am." Jack raised Bea's hand to his lips. Meeting her eyes, he brushed a kiss over her knuckles.

Bea's heart fluttered madly. If this was Jack's idea of pretending, then he was far more adept at the exercise than she was. The way he looked at her, she might almost believe that he meant it.

The other ladies observed Jack's tribute with varying degrees of dismay. All except for Miss Farraday herself who wore her perpetual mask of ladylike composure.

"Then Mrs. Dimsdale has spoken truly," Mrs. Rawson said. "You and Miss Layton are engaged to be married?"

"We are," Jack affirmed.

Miss Farraday was the first to offer Bea a smile. Unlike her mother's, it appeared to be genuine. "I congratulate you, Miss Layton."

"Thank you," Bea replied.

"And you, Colonel Beresford," Miss Farraday said to Jack. "I hope you will be very happy."

"Yes, yes," Mrs. Rawson said dismissively. "But do your parents know of this, sir? Surely Lord and Lady Allendale—"

"My parents are certain to be overjoyed, ma'am," Jack said. "They have long wished for me to be settled."

Bea wondered if that was true.

"They will surely be surprised," Mrs. Dimsdale pronounced darkly.

Mrs. Farraday stepped forward. A rigid smile graced her features. Only her eyes betrayed her lack of good humor. They were exceedingly hard. "We must act in their stead," she said, "as both companions and chaperones."

Bea felt Jack's hand tighten on hers.

"For though you might be engaged, you are not yet married," Mrs. Farraday continued. "It wouldn't be seemly if you were left too much alone with each other during the remainder of the journey. Isn't that right, Mrs. Rawson?"

"Too right," Mrs. Rawson agreed as Benjamin squirmed under her arm. "Your parents will be grateful to us, I wager, for delivering you home without the taint of scandal marring your good name."

"A generous impulse, to be sure," Jack said. "But I have no fear of scandal at this late stage. I'm a man of four and thirty, not a stripling lad."

"And I am six and twenty." Bea was amazed by the steadiness of her voice. "I know my own mind."

"As do I." Jack tucked Bea's hand in his arm. "Miss Layton will be ample company for me. You may trust that we will observe all proprieties."

"But Colonel—" Mrs. Farraday began.

"Which reminds me," Jack said, addressing Mrs. Rawson. "I understand you have a maid you might be willing to hire out for the purpose."

"Pearl?" Mrs. Rawson resettled her now thrashing little dog. "Why yes, sir."

"But *I* have been given leave to make use of her," Mrs. Dimsdale objected. "The girl is looking after my children since Miss Layton—" she broke off. "That is to say... since I find myself without a—"

"Naturally it would be my honor to loan Pearl to you for what remains of the sea voyage," Mrs. Rawson interrupted. Benjamin gave a plaintive yap. "And may I say, the very least Lord and Lady Allendale might expect from one whom I hope might dare to call herself their friend."

Bea had never witnessed such an outright display of toadying. Then again, she'd never before been in company with anyone so exalted as the son of an earl. Perhaps this sort of behavior was normal? If it was, it went a long way to explaining why Jack had been pursued so relentlessly.

"Excellent," he said. "My batman will be arranging a stateroom for Miss Layton. You may direct your maid there once all is settled."

Mrs. Rawson beamed. "I shall, sir. With my compliments."

"Ma'am." Jack inclined his head to her. "Ladies." Having effectively ended the conversation, he steered Bea away.

"But what about the children?" Mrs. Dimsdale's plaintive query sounded shrilly behind them. "Who is to look after them?"

Bea descended the stairs with Jack, unable to hear the answer to Mrs. Dimsdale's question over the roar of the wind and sea.

"I trust you've regained your appetite," Jack said cheerfully. "Because I'm famished."

## Chapter Eleven

Bea wished she could eat. But though her stomach was hollow as an empty gourd, she found herself unable to manage the smallest morsel.

Never in her life had she felt so much under a microscope. Every eye in the dining saloon seemed to be trained upon them. Some diners were sneaking fascinated looks. Others stared openly. A few were even whispering behind their hands, by heaven.

Not that Jack appeared to notice. He sat beside Bea at the linen-draped table, inhaling his enormous breakfast like a man breaking a ten-day fast. The rasher of bacon he'd heaped on his plate was gone. So too the eggs, fruit, and bread rolls.

She toyed with her own meal with her fork as she observed him from the beneath her lashes. One might think he hadn't a care in the world. And perhaps he hadn't, now that she had been enlisted to protect him from the scores of ladies who wished to trap him into marriage.

Bea wasn't entirely unsympathetic to their aims.

What woman among them could set eyes on Jack and not be lured into daydreams about having him for her own? The temptation was palpable, even for Bea. Even now, sitting beside him, subjected to only his unrelenting silence and his strongly chiseled profile.

As she looked at him, the bewildering emotions Bea had felt when he'd kissed her hand came back to torment her.

She refused to let them.

This wasn't a romance. This was only another job. She'd had enough of them over the years. Through it all she'd done whatever was required of her. This would surely be no different.

Except that she wasn't acting as a servant any longer. She was acting as a lady. Jack's chosen lady, to be precise.

Bea's stomach roiled in protest at the flagrant deception. She set down her fork, giving up on her breakfast altogether.

Across the dining saloon, the unmistakable shriek of a Dimsdale child rose above the din. "I'm not finishing *that!*" one of the twins cried. "And you can't make me!"

Bea flinched at the sound. She hadn't seen Pearl and the children when she'd entered the dining room. It had been too crowded. But Pearl had undoubtedly seen Bea.

Good lord, what must she have thought?

Bea discreetly craned her neck, scanning the other side of the room until she found Pearl seated at a low table with Lilith, Albermarle Jr., and the twins. Pearl's expression was harried as she attempted to keep the intractable brood in order.

"Can't you see we're done already?" Lilith demanded of Pearl in tones dripping with condescension. "Stupid girl!"

Bea gritted her teeth. She had wanted to be free of the

Dimsdales. But not at the expense of her friend. Her *only* friend.

Coming to a swift decision, she stood from her chair.

Jack immediately moved to rise.

"Don't trouble yourself," Bea said. "I shall be back directly." She didn't wait for Jack's objection, or his reminder that she wasn't meant to leave his side. Some things were more important than promises to pretend fiancés.

She marched across the dining saloon with single-minded intent. This time, she didn't care if every eye was upon her. She was too angry to regard it. All that mattered was Pearl.

Lilith had already risen from the table, along with Albermarle Jr. Pearl was attempting to wrangle the twins. Brent had just taken her hand when Bea approached, while Damian remained seated, smacking the flat of his spoon into his scrambled eggs, so that they splattered all about him.

"Good morning," Bea said to Pearl. "If I may intervene?"

Pearl stared at her, her black hair frizzled about her face and her dark eyes vaguely accusing.

Bea didn't wait for her friend's permission. "Put that spoon down, Damian," she commanded the twin. "*Now.* And do as Pearl tells you."

Damian stilled, visibly confused by the unfamiliar edge in Bea's voice. She'd never been permitted to address to them so forcefully when she'd been their governess. To do so would have been to risk dismissal.

"You can't tell him what to do," Lilith retorted sharply. "You're not our—"

"And you," Bea said, turning on the imperious little girl.

"Your voice can be heard all the way across the dining saloon, and on the upper deck too, I don't wonder. What do you suppose your Mama and Miss Farraday will think to hear you screaming like the veriest fishwife?"

Albermarle snickered. "A fishwife! Ha!"

Lilith's face mottled with fury. "I did not sound like a—"

"Up from your seat, Damian," Bea said. "No more dawdling, or I shall have one of the stewards carry you out like a sack of laundry."

The little boy bolted up, dropping his spoon to his plate with a clatter.

"You can't speak to us like that!" Lilith declared shrilly. "You can't—"

"Be quiet," Bea said. "Or the steward will have two children to carry out." She addressed Pearl before the little girl could reply. "After you return them to their mother, I hoped you and I might speak in our quarters."

Pearl's lips compressed as she took Damian's sticky hand. "Very well."

Bea nodded. And turning on her heel, she walked back to the table where Jack was waiting for her. He watched her come, frowning.

As she returned to her chair, he rose again with the aid of his cane, ever the gentleman, only resuming his seat once Bea was seated herself.

"What was that about?" he asked.

Bea picked up her fork. "Friendship."

A SHORT TIME LATER, ALONE WITH PEARL IN THEIR tiny cabin, Bea offered her friend a disjointed (and, admittedly, not entirely truthful) explanation of events. "So, you see," she concluded at length, "it wasn't *my* idea to commandeer you as my lady's maid. I would never have suggested—"

"Then the ladies were speaking truly?" Pearl asked. "You *are* to marry Colonel Beresford?"

She hadn't seemed to have heard any of Bea's excuses. She'd stopped listening from the moment Bea had told her that she and Jack were engaged. Anything beyond that astounding fact had instantly become superfluous to the conversation.

Bea didn't blame her friend. In truth, Bea was still rather stunned by this morning's turn of events herself. One moment she'd been alone, staring down Mrs. Dimsdale, and what promised to be a very bleak future. The next she'd had Jack at her side.

He'd be at her side still if she hadn't begged for a moment alone to speak to Pearl. Jack had agreed to it on the condition that Bea first accompany him to his cabin. Yet another reminder of the real reason for her elevation from lowly servant to much-envied fiancée. She wasn't his sweetheart, nor even his friend. She was a living, breathing barrier between Jack and those who would attempt to encroach upon him.

"But where did you—*how* did you—" Pearl faced Bea, her brows beetled as she attempted to piece the unlikely romance together. "It wasn't on those moonlight rambles of yours above deck?"

Bea sank down on the edge of her berth. She hated lying

to her friend, but saw no way around it. "It was," she said. "We've met most every night since leaving port."

Pearl's eyes widened in astonishment. "You never said!"

"I could hardly do so," Bea replied.

"But I thought—" Pearl shook her head. "It's been less than a week. How could you—?"

"I didn't intend to."

"Everyone intends to, where Colonel Beresford is concerned. They can't help themselves."

Bea didn't like what Pearl was implying. "I hope you don't class me with the Farradays and their like."

Pearl snorted. "You're a woman, aren't you?"

"I didn't pursue him. And I didn't—I would *never*— become so exalted in my opinion of myself that I'd ask a friend to be my servant."

"Why not? It's preferable to minding those evil children. And we're to have a stateroom?" Pearl brightened. "The rest of the voyage will fly by."

Some of the tension in Bea's shoulders eased. She'd been so anxious over Pearl's reaction. "Then . . . you don't mind it?"

"I shall relish it," Pearl declared. "Even if I must return to Mrs. Rawson when we arrive in France." She sank down beside Bea on the berth. Her expression was determined. "You'll still require a lady's maid once you disembark at Southampton."

Bea dropped her gaze. What could she say? That she'd no more require a maid once she was in England than she would require a wedding dress or a trousseau?

"I don't mean myself," Pearl said. "I've been with Mrs. Rawson too long to abandon her for another position. But you can't meet Colonel Beresford's family, or put up at one of their houses, without *someone* to attend you. What do you mean to do—"

"I shall cross that bridge when I come to it," Bea interrupted. "Until then, I must take each day as it comes."

And pray that she and Jack could get through them all without anyone discovering their deception, she added silently.

# Chapter Twelve

J ack leaned back in his chair as he examined the cards in his hand. Bea was seated across from him at a small, felt-topped table in the ship's gaming saloon, his half-hearted opponent in a rubber of picquet. He told himself that he didn't mind her lack of enthusiasm. Her presence had saved him from being pressed into a foursome with the Farradays and Mrs. Rawson. That alone was enough to earn Bea his endless gratitude.

"This engagement isn't half bad," he remarked.

Bea glanced up at him from over her own hand of cards. "Naturally you would say that *now*."

"I would." His mouth quirked. "I do."

She arranged her cards. "It's been but a few days."

Three days, more precisely, since their engagement had been announced.

Jack and Bea had been in company with each other for nearly every waking moment of them. Every day. Every hour. At mealtimes, during leisurely airings above deck, and smoke-filled evenings spent over cards in the gaming saloon.

They were never alone. The Rawsons, Dimsdales, Farradays, and other first-class passengers were forever circling them like sharks. Yet, through it all, Bea remained steadfast in her position. She sat primly beside Jack while he read, scribbling in her journal or attending to her sewing. She was his silent companion while he talked with any ladies and gentlemen who approached. And she was his protector, her very presence as his fiancée acting as a deterrent to those would otherwise have attempted to wheedle their way into his company, his affections, his life.

"Your point?" he asked.

"You'll feel differently by the time we're through."

"I might," he allowed. "But I doubt it."

They had but five days remaining until they arrived in England. Jack couldn't imagine growing dissatisfied with their arrangement in so short a time.

Bea didn't appear convinced. "If I were you, I'd be pining for time to myself."

"I never pine." Jack laid down a card. A troublesome thought occurred to him. "Are you?"

"Am I what?"

"Pining for time to yourself?"

She perused her hand, only half listening to him. "I take time for myself."

"In your stateroom?" he asked.

"Above deck," she said absently. "After dark. Just as I always have."

Jack's gaze jerked to hers with a startled frown. "You're still wandering the deck of the ship at night?"

"I don't wander."

That meant yes.

His frown turned into a scowl. "What the devil for?"

"Fresh air," she said as if it were the most reasonable answer in the world.

To Jack, it was anything but. "You get plenty of air. We both do. We're above deck half the day."

"Moonlight, then."

He scoffed. "Vastly overrated."

She laid down a card. "And starlight."

"For cosmic beauty, is that it?" he asked. "To ponder the mystery of the stars? Is that what I'm to believe?"

"I've told you as much," she said. "But I suppose you find it hard to believe that a mere drudge would appreciate such refined things."

Jack's brows snapped together. "That's not what I said."

"It's what you meant."

"You presume to tell me what I mean when—" He broke off, belatedly registering the interested looks of some of the other guests in the gaming saloon.

Miss Farraday and her mother were both staring in Jack's and Bea's direction from across the carpeted room. So were Mrs. Rawson and Mrs. Dimsdale. Jack even caught a furtive glance from Mr. Dimsdale who was seated round a low table, nursing his drink, with two similarly occupied gentlemen.

Jack banished the scowl from his brow. He forced himself to smile, as though the two of them were engaged in congenial conversation. "It isn't what I meant, termagant," he said quietly. "And we have an audience."

Bea's gaze flicked straight to the Farradays' table.

"Don't look," Jack advised under his breath.

Bea returned her attention to her cards. A flush of heightened color briefly darkened her cheeks. "Did I raise my voice?"

"We both did."

"Something we have in common," she observed. "We're both over passionate."

Jack suspected she was right. He hadn't realized it when he'd proposed the false engagement to her. He'd known she was starchy, of course, but he'd seen precious little of her spirit. That singular blaze that came into her face and her eyes when she was arguing against an injustice or coming to the aid of a friend.

It was really quite magnificent.

He didn't like to acknowledge just *how* magnificent.

"And I wasn't implying that you were a drudge," he added gruffly.

"What *were* you implying?" she asked.

"That a man has already tried to impose on you once during your wanderings. If I hadn't been there—"

"Well," she interrupted, "fortunately for me, you were."

"But not anymore." Jack no longer went above deck after dark. He had no need to. Thanks to Bea, he could now move about freely during the daylight hours and leave his nights for sleeping. "What do you plan to do if such an outrage should happen again?"

"I don't imagine it will," she said. "Not now I'm engaged to you."

"A drunkard who comes upon you in the moonlight won't care who you're engaged to."

"As to that—"

"Besides which," Jack continued, with fresh irritation, "I thought you only emerged at night as a respite from the children?"

"From my work, yes."

Jack had to make an effort not to scowl again. "Which

you still require, apparently." He rearranged his remaining cards with unusually brusque movements. "Tell me, do you put me in the same class as those savages?"

Her mouth tipped in the barest suggestion of a smile. "Indeed, I do not."

Jack was unmollified.

It occurred to him that, in becoming engaged to Bea, all he'd done was hire himself a vexing and rather attractive nurse. Perhaps that was how she saw their arrangement too, less as his fake fiancée and more as a paid companion to a demanding invalid.

Judging by her desire to venture above deck alone after dark, it wasn't a position she was enjoying overmuch. Though honestly, Jack reflected bitterly, he would have thought it preferable to the alternative.

"Why did you choose to become a governess?" he asked.

The question seemed to take her aback. "What?"

"Do you like children?"

She resumed perusing her cards. "I don't *dis*like them."

Under other circumstances, Jack would have laughed. But not this evening. "Then the position wasn't your heart's desire?"

"To be a governess?" She flashed him an incredulous glance. "Are you in jest?"

"I'm in earnest."

She huffed. "You must never have known any governesses."

It was a fair point.

Jack hadn't known any. Not intimately.

"My little sister had a governess. Miss Cray, her name was. A nervous little woman. She drank, I believe. But," he added, "that was my sister's doing."

Bea's hand froze midway to laying down a card. "Your sister induced her to drink?"

"My sister's *behavior* induced her to drink." Jack's mouth curled at the memory of all the shocking scrapes Kate had embroiled herself in over the years. "Kate was a hellion. She'd try the patience of a saint. My parents were at pains to constrain her behavior."

Bea played her card. "Did they succeed?"

"Lord no. Thankfully, Kate found someone she wished to marry. She's his problem now."

"And what of Miss Cray?"

"Pensioned off to a cottage on one of our estates," Jack said.

A strange expression crossed Bea's face. "That was extraordinarily kind of your family."

Jack shrugged, returning his attention to his cards. What could he say? That his father had once been something of a servant himself? An alleged bastard, raised as a stable boy on Jack's mother's childhood estate?

It was a family scandal, rumors of which had still been plaguing the Beresfords at the time Jack joined the army. Not at all the sort of thing a chap should be sharing with a stranger. Even if that stranger *was* his fake fiancée.

"We Beresfords aren't typically top lofty sorts," he said instead. "Not unless we have to be."

"Does anyone *have* to be?" Bea wondered.

"Arrogance has its uses. One never knows when one might have to deliver an edict." Jack paused. "By the by, I'll be joining you on your midnight rambles this evening."

Bea cast him another glance over the top of her cards. There was a look in her eyes that was difficult to read.

Jack's stomach tensed. "I trust you don't object?"

"On the contrary," she said at last. "I should be glad of your company."

# Chapter Thirteen

*Later that night . . .*

J ack grimaced as Maberly massaged salve into Jack's injured leg. It was all part of the treatment the surgeon in Cairo had prescribed—medicated salve, massage, and applications of ice and heat, to be administered first thing in the morning and before retiring at night. Maberly had learned the basics of it before Jack had been discharged from the hospital in Cairo. Still...

"Must you be so bloody rough?" Jack asked crossly. "You're not tenderizing a piece of mutton for the table."

Maberly made no reply, but his fingers kneaded Jack's spasmed muscles with a fraction less pressure. A lantern hung behind him, illuminating the periphery of the cabin, but leaving the rest in shadows.

It was nearly eleven o'clock. Almost time for Jack to meet Bea above deck for their promised rendezvous in the moonlight.

But practical matters must inevitably come first.

Jack leaned back in his berth, closing his eyes rather than witness his batman's medical ministrations. All things considered, he preferred not to look at his leg. Whenever he did, it never failed to lower his spirits. And he wanted his spirits up tonight when he met Bea on the deck.

"You're awfully silent this evening," he remarked to Maberly. "Am I meant to take it as censure?"

Maberly didn't answer.

Which was answer enough in itself.

"It's been three days," Jack said. "I'd have thought that ample time to smooth your ruffled feathers where Miss Layton's concerned."

Maberly made a chuffing noise, somewhere between a scoff and a grunt.

Jack cracked an eye open to glare at his batman. They'd been through too much together over the years not to speak plainly. "If you've something to say, then say it and be done," he commanded. "I won't have you glowering all over the ship, telegraphing your displeasure to all and sundry. This engagement is meant to solve problems, not create new ones."

"*Your* problems?" Maberly inquired darkly.

"And hers," Jack said. "It was the only way I could help her."

"Don't know why it's up to you to help a governess you met on a ruddy ship," Maberly grumbled. "Not your business, I'd have said."

"Is it her you disapprove of?" Jack asked. Both of his eyes were open now. "Or merely the haste of the announcement?"

Maberly straightened. He wiped his hands on a towel. "I disapprove of the entire scheme."

"A scheme," Jack repeated. "That's what you call it?"

Maberly frowned. "Isn't it?"

Jack felt a flinch of conscience. He sat up from his berth. "If it is, it's not the sort that will hurt anyone."

The batman uttered another disbelieving grunt. As he helped Jack dress, his dour expression left no doubt as to how he felt about Jack's engagement to Bea. "Chill night tonight," he said, assisting Jack into his coat. "Better you should spend it resting your leg than traipsing about."

"Probably." But Jack had already told Bea he'd be meeting her. A little cold wasn't going to stop him. Speaking of which...

"Where are those gifts I bought in Cairo?" Jack asked.

Maberly's forehead scrunched. "Them packages for her ladyship and your sisters?"

"Those are the ones." Jack had bought an excess of presents for his mother and Kate, and for his sisters-in-law, Hannah and Meg. Not to mention the countless trifles he'd purchased for his nieces and nephews.

Maberly grudgingly removed one of Jack's leather cases from a short stack of luggage on the opposite wall. He sat it on a chair and opened it. "They're here, sir."

Jack came to stand in front of the open case. His weight resting on his cane, he rummaged through the paper-and-twine-wrapped parcels within. There were several of them that were soft and relatively flat. He picked one up. "This is one of Kate's, I believe," he said. "She won't miss it."

Maberly's face darkened with unspoken censure.

Jack paid him no heed. Tucking the parcel in his coat, he exited his cabin in search of Bea.

The sea air was indeed chill tonight, stinging his face as he ascended to the upper deck. He didn't like to think of

Bea, standing at the rail in her thin gown and threadbare shawl.

Yet, it was precisely where he found her. There, in the moonlight, hands at the rail as she stared out at the stars.

"You've anticipated me," he said.

She cast him a glance over her shoulder. "You said you'd be joining me. I took you at your word."

He limped up to the rail. "Have you been here long?"

"Not long, no." Her mouth curved in a fleeting smile. "I've been pondering the mystery of the stars."

He inwardly winced to hear the sardonic words he'd uttered in the gaming saloon volleyed back at him. "Ah."

"Is that what *you* do when you look at the night sky?" she asked. "Consider its mystery?"

"I don't know that I've ever spent much time looking upward," Jack admitted. "There's too much to keep my attention here on the ground."

"Indeed," Bea said. "It's only dreamers who have cause to stare at the stars."

"You presume I'm not a dreamer?"

Her slim shoulder lifted in a faint shrug. "If you already have everything you want, you have no need to dream."

A flicker of irritation took Jack unaware. "What makes you think I already have everything I want?"

"Don't you?" she asked.

Jack didn't answer.

He *couldn't* answer.

He had wealth and position, it was true. He had the love of his family. The admiration of the soldiers that served under his command. But was that everything?

Was it enough?

"I'd not have characterized you as a dreamer either," he said instead.

"I'm not," she replied matter-of-factly. "It was my mother who dreamed." She drew her shawl tighter around herself. "She had a tradition. Every night, without fail, she would venture out into our garden and make a wish on the evening star."

"A dreamer, indeed."

"Not outwardly. She was a practical woman in every other respect, but at her heart, she held a belief in magic." Bea cast him another glance. "Not real magic, of course. But the power that exists for good things to happen in the bleakest circumstances."

"Were her circumstances bleak?" Jack asked.

"I didn't think so. But... I suppose she wanted more."

"Is that why you're forever searching the night sky? Making wishes on stars in memory of your mother?"

"Not only for her," Bea said. "I make them for myself too."

Jack studied her face. When first they'd met, he had thought her younger than her six and twenty years. And she *was* young in comparison to him. Yet there were already fine lines at the corners of her eyes and a certain world weariness at the back of her gaze. She'd known hardship, loneliness. It was written there in her features if one troubled to look for it.

He hated that for her. That she'd ever experienced a moment of anguish or despair. It wasn't right that she should have suffered on account of people like the Dimsdales, or for any other reason.

"Now *that* I find hard to believe," he said.

"Why?" she asked. "Because I'm a cynic?"

"I'd have said sensible."

"I hope I am sensible."

"Yet you make wishes."

She smiled slightly. There was a glimmer of ruefulness in the expression. Bitterness too, so faint it might have been a trick of the moonlight. "For all my cynicism, I suppose I want to believe what my mother believed. That something wonderful can happen if you only have the courage to ask for it. To wish for it."

As she spoke, a delicate tremor went through her frame.

Jack regarded her with concern. "You're shivering."

Bea dismissed the observation as though it were of no account to her. "It *is* a little cold this evening," she allowed. "But I shall be all right."

"With that meager shawl?" Jack scoffed. "Here. You might like this better." He withdrew the parcel from his coat and offered it to her.

She looked at the package with swift suspicion. "What is it?"

"Nothing outrageous. Just a trifle I picked up during my travels. I have a trunkful of them in my cabin." He pressed it to her. "Take it. It's a purely practical item, I assure."

Bea reluctantly accepted the gift. Her fingers nimbly removed the twine and the paper wrappings, revealing the vibrantly colored shawl within. It was sky-blue, with a border of embroidered flowers and leaves.

Jack recalled encountering it at a bazaar during his first outing after his surgery. He'd thought it an uncommonly pretty pattern. One that didn't entirely suit his mother, sister, or sisters-in-law. For some reason, he'd bought it anyway.

Bea's gaze jolted to his. "I can't accept this! It's cashmere!"

"Nonsense," Jack said. "I won't allow my fiancée to catch a chill above deck."

"But I'm *not* your fiancée, as you very well know. It's all just playacting."

Jack smiled, amused by her maidenish indignance. "In that case, you may consider this part of your costuming."

She shook her head, even as she touched the shawl with her fingers. A vaguely wistful expression came into her eyes.

Looking at her in that moment, Jack could readily believe that she was a dreamer like her mother.

"Come," he said. "Put it on before you catch your death."

"I'm not likely to," she said. "I have a very robust constitution."

"Bea, must you always be so literal? And ungrateful too, I might add. Every time I attempt to be gallant—"

"Oh, very well." She grudgingly slipped her old shawl from her shoulders.

Jack took it from her. He thrust it into his pocket for safekeeping as Bea unfolded the new shawl and draped it around herself.

The rich colors of the cashmere transformed her in an instant, enlivening the whole of her person and making her eyes shine like twin jewels.

She glared at him. "There. Are you satisfied?"

Jack swallowed hard. "I'm exceedingly satisfied," he managed.

"Who did you really buy it for?" she asked.

"No one," he said. "I simply thought it beautiful. I

figured it would do for one of the many females in my life. And it has."

"Is that what I am now? A female in your life?"

"Does the thought repel you?"

"No, I..." Bea's words trailed away as he reached to adjust a fold of her shawl. "That is..."

Jack's knuckles quite unintentionally brushed over the wool-encased curve of her bosom.

His pulse quaked.

"What do you wish for?" he asked abruptly. "When you make your wishes on the evening star?"

"I can't tell you that," she replied. There was a husky catch in her voice that made his already simmering blood catch fire.

"Why not?"

"If I did, they wouldn't come true."

Jack bent his head to hers; closer, closer. Heaven knew what he was thinking. Nothing, very likely. He seemed to be operating purely on instinct. *Masculine* instinct, driven by the moon and the stars, and how surprisingly lovely Bea was beneath them in the shawl that had so obviously been meant for her.

"Are they likely to come true, these wishes you make?" he asked.

Her lashes lowered. "One of them already has," she confessed.

And he kissed her.

## Chapter Fourteen

Bea inhaled an astonished breath. She didn't know why she was surprised. Jack's intention had been clear from the moment he'd bent his head to hers. But it hadn't seemed real, for all that. Here beneath the stars, with the sea lapping below, and the deck rolling gently beneath her feet. Indeed, it all felt rather too much like a dream.

Until Jack's lips captured hers.

*That* was when she started. For there was nothing dreamlike about his kiss. It was warm and firm, and unmistakably real.

Bea stood there, for an instant—the *barest* instant—feeling time stand still between them. She was stricken by a sensation of utter disbelief. Too stunned to protest, too flustered to move.

And then her mouth trembled beneath his, her lips parting on a breathless word. To her consternation, that word wasn't stop.

*"Jack,"* she whispered.

He curved his hand around her neck in answer, kissing her again.

This time, Bea kissed him back.

Jack made a low sound in his throat as his mouth shaped to hers, returning her kiss. Deepening it.

Another tremor went through Bea's frame. It had nothing to do with the weather.

*Gracious.*

He was *good* at this. Doubtless he'd done it before. The thought entered her head only to leave it a split second later, lost amid the rush of sensation inspired by his warmth, his touch, his breath.

Her knees quaked. She brought her hands to his chest to steady herself. She couldn't recall if they'd ever been this close before. She was certain she'd have remembered it if they had. He was so devastatingly tall and solid. So relentlessly male. His very nearness was intoxicating to her; the heat of his body, the breadth of his shoulders, the fragrance of his cologne.

*Good heavens.*

*Had* she wished for this?

She didn't know for certain. All she knew was that being in his company for the past three days, pretending to be his devoted fiancée, had taken an unaccountable toll. The pantomime had eaten away at her restraint. Had played havoc with her heart. Her soul.

How could she look at him hour upon hour, talk with him, dine with him, be the recipient of his many gentlemanly considerations, and not be moved by it all? She was not, after all, made of stone.

Her fingers curled into the fabric of his wool coat. She

realized, with vague alarm, that she was clinging to him. All but embracing him.

He didn't embrace her in return, but his fingers were a hot brand at her neck, making her heartbeat gallop as wildly as a horse bolting from the too-restrictive confines of its stable.

"A bit awkward," Jack murmured against her mouth.

Bea stiffened. "Me?"

He stroked her nape. "Not you. *This*." He gave a humorless chuckle. "Me."

Bea drew back from him a fraction, incredulous. "You call this awkward?"

"I do," he said. "I'm not accustomed to—" He stopped, uttering another wry huff. "I haven't been with anyone like this since I fell at Mohammerah."

Bea began to understand. She searched his face. "You mean... you haven't kissed anyone since your injury?"

Jack's expression betrayed a flicker of bitterness. "It occurs to me that it might be easier sitting down. For one thing, I could dispense with this." He shot a dark glance at his cane. "For another..." His eyes returned to hers. The bitterness was gone. In its place was a gleam of gentle amusement. "You might be in less danger of falling into a swoon."

Heat rose in Bea's cheeks. Her hands fell from his chest, leaving his coat creased where she'd clenched it with her fingers. "I was *not* in danger of swooning," she informed him.

He smiled. "No? I must have been mistaken."

She stepped back forcing his hand to fall from her neck. "I daresay you're used to ladies swooning when you kiss them."

"If they didn't," he said, "I'd think myself a very dull fellow indeed."

Bea snorted. "Vanity, thy name is Beresford."

"Just as I warned you. But it wasn't—"

"What wasn't it?" she asked, cutting him off.

Jack's expression grew serious. "I'm not a scoundrel, Bea."

"No?" She touched the soft cashmere of her shawl. Never in her life had she possessed anything so fine. "Then, that kiss... It wasn't payment for this?"

A frown darkened his gaze. "Is that what you think of me?"

"What else should I think? In one breath you give me an expensive gift. In another you kiss me. The two events—"

"Are mutually exclusive," he said. "I beg your pardon for the offense, but..." He smiled again with quicksilver humor. "You must allow that the inducement was extraordinary."

Bea's eyes narrowed. She had never considered herself a temptation before. Let alone one that was impossible to resist. "I'm not much of an inducement."

"You are to me," Jack said.

She took a step back from him. It was one thing to be kissed by a gentleman. It was quite another to be teased by him. "You don't mean that."

"Why wouldn't I mean it? I've been in company with you a great deal since we became engaged—"

"We're not—"

"We *are*," he said. "And I enjoy being with you. Anyone would."

Bea shook her head. The farther she moved away from him, the more swiftly reality returned to her. She couldn't be doing this. Kissing him. Wanting him. Daring to dream that they might—

*No.*

She wouldn't allow herself to follow that thread. It could lead to only one destination. And it wasn't the marriage altar. It was directly to her own ruination.

"You don't know me, Jack," she said.

"But I do," he said. "I know that you're daring. I know that you're loyal. That you have a keen sense of justice. That you loved your mother. I know that you make wishes on stars."

A lump formed in Bea's throat. "I wasn't aware you were keeping a catalog."

"And you're not?"

"It's not the same," she said.

Jack was something worth knowing. A gentleman of importance. Of wealth, property, and pedigree. While, she...

"In any event," she added brusquely, "it hardly matters. We've nearly reached Marseilles. In but a few more days, we shall arrive in England and go our separate ways. I shan't ever see you again. Unless—"

"Unless you'd *like* to see me again," Jack suggested.

Bea's brows lowered. "I was going to say, unless I should happen to be employed by a near neighbor of yours."

"Ah." Jack's smile faded. "Now *that* might be awkward."

"And we don't want that," Bea said. "Better we should keep to our agreement in public."

"What about in private?" he asked.

"We must be friends," she said. "And nothing more."

"And friends don't kiss friends, presumably," he said.

"Not like that."

"I see. What about gifts? Can a friend give his friend a shawl?"

Bea's throat constricted. The answer was no. Not if that friend was a gentlemen friend, and not if the recipient was an unmarried young lady.

But they'd already bent some of the rules. Surely it could do no harm to bend them a little more in this respect?

"I suppose a friend could," she said slowly. "But only as you described earlier."

"I can't recall what I described," Jack replied frankly. "Everything before I kissed you is somewhat of a blur."

Heat crept into Bea's cheeks. "You called it costuming for my role," she reminded him.

Jack leaned more heavily on his cane. "So I did."

"Which means I may wear it for the remainder of our journey, but..." Bea hesitated to utter the words. She wanted so badly to keep her present. "But... I must return it to you when we part."

Jack accepted her judgment as though he'd been expecting it. "Very well. If that's how you prefer it."

It wasn't how Bea preferred it. But what could she say? More to the point, what could she do? A governess had only her reputation to recommend her. Without that, she had nothing.

No. There was no more to be said.

She glumly permitted Jack to accompany her back to her stateroom. They didn't speak again. Not on any topics worth mentioning. He remarked on the weather, and the calmness of the sea, filling up the silence until he deposited her safely at the door of her cabin.

Only then did he look at her, addressing her with uncommon seriousness. "You never told me which of your wishes came true," he said.

"No, I didn't," Bea replied as she opened her door.

And she never would.

# Chapter Fifteen

*Marseilles to Calais*
*April 1858*

Bea sank down on a bench at the edge of the railway platform amid the swirling smoke and steam. Pearl took a seat beside her, Bea's small leather traveling valise cradled in her arms. After docking in Marseilles, they'd wasted no time in getting themselves, and their luggage, to the station. It was going to be many hours to Calais by train. And several more across the Channel by steamship. They couldn't afford to dawdle.

Not all of the passengers had been so impatient to resume their journey. Several had taken rooms at local hotels, eager to rest and—as they put it—regain their land legs. Bea had hoped the Dimsdales would be among them, but it wasn't to be. No sooner had she sat down than they stalked past her on their way to the ticket office.

Mrs. Dimsdale was shepherding her children, with little success. "We must find a servant to look after them," she was saying to her husband. "Anyone woman will do. Even if she *is* a Frenchwoman."

"Yes, my dear," Mr. Dimsdale replied. "Whatever you will."

They neither of them spared a glance in Bea's direction. It was as though she didn't exist. Only Lilith dared look at her, her mouth sullen, and her gaze glinting with mingled scorn and awe.

"You have achieved the impossible in her eyes," Pearl remarked once the family had disappeared from sight.

"Have I?" Bea asked absently. She wasn't entirely paying attention to her friend. She was too focused on Jack.

He stood a short distance away, dressed for travel in a heavy wool coat, black gloves, and a tall black hat. He was speaking with a raven-haired gentleman that Bea had never seen before.

The man's stern face was partially concealed by the upturned collar of his greatcoat and the hat he wore tipped low over his brow. He seemed to be glaring at Jack for some reason.

Not that one would know it by Jack's easy demeanor. He was untroubled as ever, his weight balanced on his cane, and his mouth curved in its perpetual wry smile of amusement.

As she looked at him, Bea's stomach quivered with butterflies. The same wretched winged irritants that had been plaguing her ever since their ill-advised kiss on the deck of the Pera. It had been days since that unfortunate encounter. Every one of which she'd spent in Jack's company.

His behavior toward her had been perfectly gentlemanly. His aspect civil. His conversation friendly. Practically brotherly.

Or at least, how Bea imagined a brother might be.

And yet...

Every time she looked at him, she was thinking about that wretched kiss. Both regretting that it had happened, and regretting that it could never happen again.

"You have snared a Beresford," Pearl said.

Bea flashed her friend a repressive glance. "What does an eleven-year-old girl know about snaring anyone?"

"It's all she's heard from the ladies since we set out from Bombay, how exceptional a catch Colonel Beresford is. And you're the one who caught him."

"I don't know about that," Bea said under her breath.

"*I* know," Pearl said. "I'm sorry we must part. I'd have liked to see you married and settled in your grand estate in the west country." She smiled. "I'd ask you to write to me if I thought you'd be willing."

A leaden weight formed in Bea's chest. She recognized it as guilt. "Why wouldn't I be willing?"

"The daughter-in-law of an earl can't be corresponding with a maidservant she met on the crossing," Pearl replied matter-of-factly.

Bea hadn't thought she could feel any worse. "Of course I shall write you," she said. "The moment I'm settled, I'll send word to you at..."

"Mrs. Rawson's residence in Hampshire," Pearl supplied. "The Birches, it's called."

Across the platform, Mrs. Rawson emerged from the telegraph office as though their conversation had summoned her. Benjamin was on his lead ahead of her, and Mrs.

Farraday and her daughter were close behind. Like Bea and Jack, the three ladies had elected to book passage on the next train to Calais rather than take rooms in a hotel for the night.

Catching sight of Bea, Mrs. Rawson raised her kid-gloved hand in greeting. "Miss Layton!" she called. "Well met."

Bea suppressed a sigh as the three ladies came to join them.

Standing as a barrier between Jack and his encroachers hadn't turned out to be as simple an endeavor as she'd originally hoped it would be. For one thing, the fact of Jack's engagement to Bea did little to keep those encroachers at bay. They were still there, persistently pressing their acquaintance, and—in Mrs. Farraday's case—forever reminding Bea how ludicrous it was that a drab creature like her had supplanted Mrs. Farraday's beautiful daughter in Jack's affections.

It was trying at the best of times, but after so many days at sea, Bea was tired of it. She nevertheless grudgingly rose to greet them.

"Mrs. Rawson. Mrs. Farraday. Miss Farraday." Bea inclined her head.

Mrs. Rawson came to a halt, struggling with Benjamin. The little dog continued pulling wildly on his lead. It was obvious why his owner preferred to carry him. When left to his own devices he was barely civilized.

Setting aside Bea's valise, Pearl scurried forward. "Shall I help you with Benjamin, Mrs. Rawson?"

"Yes, do," Mrs. Rawson said. "What a relief it will be to have you resume your duties!"

Bea opened her mouth to offer a word of thanks, or

possibly apology. It was, after all, because of her that Mrs. Rawson had been deprived of Pearl during the voyage.

Mrs. Rawson forestalled her. "Not that I begrudged your use of her. A young lady, newly betrothed, can't be sleeping alone in a stateroom without a servant to attend her. What would people say? No, my dear. So long as we were on the Pera, I considered it my sacred duty to see that all proprieties were observed on your behalf."

"You are too kind," Bea said stiffly. "But really—"

"And it *was* only for the length of the sea voyage. I managed well enough without her, as you see. Though I won't claim it has been easy." Mrs. Rawson addressed Pearl. "Don't let him get free of you! We'd never find him again in such a crush."

Pearl picked up the struggling little dog in her arms. She scrunched her eyes shut, giggling as he licked her face. "Be still, Benjamin," she chided. "I don't require your kisses."

Mrs. Rawson and Miss Farraday smiled and tittered at the dog's antics.

Mrs. Farraday's face, by contrast, remained cold and markedly unfriendly. She wore a dove-gray poplin traveling dress and matching silk-trimmed casaque, an ensemble rivaled in its stylishness only by that worn by her daughter. "Miss Layton," she said. "You amaze me."

Bea returned the woman's gaze, steeling herself for what was sure to be an insult. "Ma'am?"

"I declare, since the morning your engagement to Colonel Beresford was so scandalously announced, I have not seen you even once outside of his company. Yet here you are." Mrs. Farraday looked around Bea in mock amazement. "And Colonel Beresford is nowhere to be found."

"He is there behind you, ma'am," Bea said. "Speaking to that tall gentleman."

Mrs. Farraday turned to look, along with Miss Farraday and Mrs. Rawson.

Jack's position had briefly been blocked by a cart holding a towering stack of cases. But the cart was gone now, and Jack could be seen quite clearly. He was still in conversation with the raven-haired man. An unpleasant conversation by the look of it.

"Upon my word," Mrs. Rawson said. "Is that the soldier who was taken prisoner during the uprising? Captain Thornhill, or whatever he's called?"

Mrs. Farraday was temporarily diverted. "The man who was tortured?"

"It must be," Mrs. Rawson said. "Though you can't see the burns he suffered from here, can you?"

Mrs. Farraday's lips pursed in a moue of distaste. "I thank God for it. Such a horrible sight isn't fit for the company of ladies."

Bea exchanged a glance with Pearl. She'd told Bea that some of the soldiers traveling on the Pera had been grievously injured, but she'd said nothing about the specifics.

"I expect Colonel Beresford is directing the frightful fellow to another carriage," Mrs. Farraday said. "He, of all men, knows the duty that is owed to ladies of quality. When first we met in Delhi, he was always watching over us. Wasn't he, Rowena?"

"Yes, Mama," Miss Farraday replied dutifully.

Mrs. Farraday turned to Bea, her face hardening to marble. "And now it's you who is watching over him. Strange, isn't it? One would think you didn't trust him out of your sight."

"It is difficult to be out of each other's sight on a ship," Bea said. "Or on a train."

"The first-class carriage, naturally." Mrs. Farraday's eyes glinted with a sharp flicker of anger. "I wonder, Miss Layton, if you are quite accustomed to traveling first class?"

"What my mother means," Miss Farraday interjected, "is that we've been worried about you acclimating to your new style of life."

Bea leveled her gaze at Miss Farraday. The young lady's outward manner was, as always, perfectly agreeable. But there was an almost imperceptible edge to her words, as razor-fine as a delicately sharpened blade.

For the first time, it occurred to Bea that Miss Farraday might have more in common with her mother than Bea had previously credited.

"If there are any difficulties," Bea told her, "I'm sure my fiancé will apprise me of them."

"Oh no, no," Mrs. Rawson protested. "A gentleman is not the one to look to for advice. You must leave that to the ladies. And to your friends in particular." She slipped her hand through Bea's arm as though they were intimates. "How much do you know about the Beresford family, Miss Layton? You have not met them before, I gather."

"No, I haven't," Bea admitted.

And she wasn't going to meet them now, either.

But Mrs. Rawson and the others didn't know that.

"Allow me to enlighten you." Mrs. Rawson dropped her voice. "The Earl of Allendale is one of the wealthiest gentlemen in the West Country. One of the largest land-holders, as well. And his countess! Margaret Honeywell, as was. Rich in her own right, and a famous beauty too, with a reputation for setting the fashion."

"A reputation all of the Beresfords share," Mrs. Farraday said coolly. "I wager Colonel Beresford's sister, Lady Katherine, wouldn't be caught dead in last season's silks or velvets. Let alone a drab dress of faded wool."

Bea suppressed a burning flare of self-consciousness. Her own dress was faded wool. Several years old, and lacking all adornment. An embarrassment, surely, as far as dresses went, if she'd actually been planning to meet Jack's family.

"And his older brother, Viscount St. Clare," Mrs. Rawson continued. "Always perfectly attired, down to the diamond pin in his neckcloth."

"You might consider purchasing your trousseau here in France," Miss Farraday suggested to Bea. "My mother and I, and Mrs. Rawson, will be stopping in Paris. If you joined us, you could have some new dresses made before you meet Lord and Lady Allendale."

"An excellent idea," Mrs. Rawson said. "No lady with the least sensibility can tolerate an overnight journey on a train with no sleeper carriage. You would have to sleep sitting up—a wretched state of affairs. No, my dear. Far better you should break your journey in Paris. I shall take you to the shops myself. I'm sure Mrs. Farraday would be happy to entertain Colonel Beresford in your absence."

"It would be my distinct pleasure," Mrs. Farraday said. Her eyes were fixed on Bea with all the subtlety of a hunting hawk eying a wayward mouse.

Bea extricated her arm from Mrs. Rawson's grasp. "You are all very kind," she said. "But I'm afraid Colonel Beresford and I haven't the time to stop in Paris. We plan on traveling straight through to Calais."

Even if that meant traveling straight through the night. Even if it meant sleeping sitting up.

"Plans can be changed," Mrs. Farraday said.

Pearl flashed Bea an encouraging look. *Yes, do stop in Paris*, it seemed to say. *Remain with us a little longer. Enjoy your new position to the utmost.*

The guilty weight in Bea's chest grew heavier still.

What would Pearl think if she knew that Bea's present position was, in fact, almost identical to her former one? Indeed, it was worse, for then she'd had a job and now she had none. Unless one counted her role as Jack's fake fiancée as employment. And it couldn't be, for there was no payment involved.

Bea swallowed the acrid taste in her mouth. Across the platform, Jack finished his conversation with Captain Thornhill, and headed toward her. They were so near to the end of this ruse. She had only to stay the course a little longer. "These plans can't, regrettably," she said. "As I'm sure Colonel Beresford can tell you."

Jack approached with a questioning smile. "What can I tell you, ladies?"

"Miss Layton claims that you haven't the time to stop over in Paris," Mrs. Rawson replied. "Though we've been making every effort to persuade her."

"Miss Layton is correct," Jack said. "I'm anxious to see my family, and to get back to my estate. Paris will have to wait."

Mrs. Rawson smiled broadly. "Your family will be equally eager to see you, I'm sure. And to meet Miss Layton."

Bea took refuge in silence, occupying herself with smoothing her skirts and adjusting her mantle. She told herself that she was glad she wouldn't have to meet Jack's family. If they were all truly so beautiful and fashionable, they'd surely have no great tolerance for her and her short-comings.

"Indeed," Jack said. He caught Bea's eye. "I have our tickets, and the luggage has all been loaded. If you're quite ready? The train will be leaving shortly, and we've a long journey ahead of us."

"Yes, of course." Bea accepted his proffered arm.

Pearl remained behind, cradling Benjamin against her chest. She gave Bea a small, parting smile.

Bea smiled in return, silently renewing her promise to write to Pearl.

"I will pray that you'll change your mind," Mrs. Rawson called after them. "It's a long way to Paris."

"A very long way," Mrs. Farraday echoed. "Much can happen between now and then."

# Chapter Sixteen

"I'm not changing my mind," Jack said the moment they were safely ensconced in their compartment. He and Bea were alone, with Maberly having been relegated to a lower-class carriage along with the servants of the other first-class passengers.

"I'm aware," Bea said.

Jack set his cane down against the seat beside him. He was feeling a trifle gray around the gills. Too much time on that dratted ship, he suspected. And too much time spent putting weight on his leg since they'd arrived in Marseilles. He was meant to exercise it, not push it past the bounds of all bearing. His knee and calf were throbbing.

It hadn't helped that he'd stood on the platform for far too long trying to talk sense into Captain Thornhill.

A useless proposition.

Thornhill had rejected all Jack's offers of assistance. He'd also rather rudely declined Jack's invitation to join him and Bea in their compartment. The man was unrelentingly stubborn about maintaining his solitude. He had a private compartment of his own, a valet to see to his needs, and a hired groom looking after his horse. It was more than sufficient, or so he claimed.

Jack had been loath to believe him. He knew only too well how traumatic injuries could color one's perspective. The idea of any soldier suffering as Thornhill likely was didn't sit well with Jack. His mood wasn't very congenial as a result.

Then again, it hadn't been congenial since he'd kissed Bea that night on the deck.

Jack regarded her with a brooding frown. He'd originally thought that time and distance would put their relationship back on a steady footing. Instead, he'd hour-by-hour found himself watching her when she wasn't aware of it, trying to puzzle out what she was thinking about their arrangement. About him.

All these days later, he was none the wiser. His little governess was a vault when she chose to be. He was rather impressed by her self-possession, even as it nettled him.

"You don't want to stop in Paris, do you?" he asked.

Bea settled in her seat next to him. "What would be the purpose? Lest you forget, I haven't actually got a trousseau to purchase."

Jack's frown deepened. "No. I suppose not."

She arranged the folds of her full skirts. "Who was that gentleman you were speaking with on the platform?"

"Thornhill? What about him?"

"Mrs. Rawson said he was a prisoner during the rebellion. That he'd been tortured."

"He was," Jack said. "I asked him to join us. I thought he might benefit from our company."

To her credit, Bea didn't look appalled by the idea. "I wasn't aware you knew any of the other soldiers on board."

"I don't. Thornhill and I first met when we boarded the ship in Alexandria. He's kept to himself since then. I've tried to draw him out, with no success."

"You feel sorry for him."

"It's not pity," Jack said. "It's empathy. When one is hurt, one often turns inward. It's not the wisest course."

"Perhaps he simply prefers his own company," Bea said. "Many people do."

Jack wondered if she was one of them. "There are other things to buy in Paris besides a trousseau," he said.

Her hands stilled for a moment as she finished smoothing her skirts. "I don't doubt it. But stopping for a pleasure jaunt was never part of our plan. You said from the beginning that we'd be traveling straight through."

"So I did," Jack acknowledged. "Speaking of our plan..."

She turned to him fully, catching the note of hesitation in his voice. "What's wrong?"

"Nothing's wrong."

Except that he was going to have to leave her in Southampton, unchaperoned, without a maid or companion to see to her safety.

The plan had seemed reasonable enough when he'd first proposed it. Governesses and women of the servant class frequently traveled alone when taking up positions in new towns. There was nothing out of the ordinary in it.

Even so...

"When we reach Southampton, you must allow me to choose the hotel that you'll stay in," he said.

"Does it matter?" she asked.

"I want you somewhere safe and respectable, where no

harm will come to you, not at some coaching inn filled with dissolute sailors and rabble."

"I'm not unaccustomed to rabble."

"Nevertheless," Jack said. "You will do as I say and remain in your room until you hear from me."

He had no sooner uttered the words, than he suppressed a wince.

Good Lord. He sounded rather horrifyingly like his brother, James. Just as top lofty and insufferable.

"Shall I, indeed?" Bea questioned in a peculiarly neutral tone.

Jack didn't like the sound of it any better than he'd liked the sound of his own words. He didn't let it stop him. "The instant I have your reference, and the direction of somewhere you might find suitable employment, I'll send it to you express."

"You won't deliver it yourself?"

"It would take too long," he said.

And it would be too painful. Saying goodbye to her. Knowing their mutual scheme had officially come to an end. That he'd likely never see her again.

Jack wasn't sure he could do it.

Not to mention his leg would hardly be up to the challenge after having just travelled all the way from Southampton to Somerset.

"I see." Bea folded her hands in her lap. A resigned look came over her. It was gone as quickly as it came, replaced by an expression of implacable resolve. "Well, I expect I shall be safe enough in an English hotel, providing I keep my door locked and don't take my meals in the public dining room."

Jack's brows lowered. The prospect of leaving her alone in such an establishment was becoming less and less appealing. "Perhaps Mrs. Rawson can be convinced to relinquish Pearl to us?"

"And further embroil her in our deception?" Bea scoffed. "No thank you. I've risked her reputation quite enough. Henceforth, I shall risk only mine." She lifted her traveling valise onto her lap. "I only wonder if it was worth it."

Jack's eyes narrowed. "For yourself?"

"For both of us," she said. "Now it's nearly over, how much good did it really do to have me as your protector on the Pera?"

Jack set a hand on the curved handle of his cane. He was tempted to answer her question with a jest, or perhaps with only his silence. But he and Bea were past the point of prevarication. "Do you see this cane?"

"What about it?" she asked.

Jack lifted it for her perusal. "I know many injured men who can walk without one, albeit with great difficulty. But I've just had surgery. Without *this*, I can't walk at all. What do you imagine would have happened if Mrs. Farraday had stolen it while I was preoccupied reading in some remote nook on the ship, or while I was dozing in the sunshine on the deck?"

Bea's lips parted in astonishment at the suggestion. "Surely she wouldn't—"

"Oh, but she would," Jack assured her. "And then, when I was trapped, unable to remove myself from a potentially sticky situation, who do you imagine might have appeared in the seat beside me, in some isolated place, where our very presence alone together would be sufficient to constitute a compromising situation?"

Bea stared at him. "Not Miss Farraday?"

"Exactly Miss Farraday," Jack said unequivocally.

Bea shook her head. "But she's never behaved in a mercenary manner. Not to you. Not so far as I've seen. Indeed, she's never seemed to have a genuine interest in you at all."

"Oh, I don't say that she likes me of her own accord. I'm not *that* vain. But she's young and obedient, and she's been brought up by her mother to do whatever's necessary to achieve their ends. If her mother told her to join me in a darkened ship's saloon, you can bet Miss Farraday would do it, and she wouldn't lose a second."

The look of disbelief in Bea's eyes faded. "Until today, I'd have said that Miss Faraday wasn't of the same mind as her mother. But the way she spoke to me on the platform... There was something in her tone that put me on my guard. It made me fear I'd misjudged her."

"Her mother had doubtless pressured her to persuade us to stop with them in Paris," Jack said. "Told her it was their last chance or some such rot."

Bea searched his face. "Is it true that she and her daughter pursued you to Cairo when you went there to have your surgery?"

"She did," Jack said somberly. "I heard about it after the fact."

It had been enough to send a chill down his spine. It was one thing to be hunted so relentlessly when he had the capacity to outmaneuver his pursuers, and quite another when he was drugged and helpless.

"How did you manage—"

"Pure luck. She couldn't find the correct hospital. By the time she did, I had already gone. But I knew I'd encounter her again on the steamer out of Alexandria. I had two choices, either wait for the next ship, or employ evasive maneuvers."

"A false name," Bea said.

"For a start."

"Self-imposed confinement to your quarters."

"That too."

She gave him an arch look. "A fake fiancée."

His mouth hitched. "A stroke of genius on my part, I must say."

"But not part of your original plan?"

"God no. It never occurred to me at all until I met you." He paused. "And yes, to answer your question. It was worth it."

BEA WASN'T UNACCUSTOMED TO LENGTHY journeys. During all her years in India, and throughout her various positions as governess, she had traversed the length and breadth of the continent by carriage, train, dak cart, and palanquin. A rail journey from Marseilles to Calais was nothing in comparison.

Except for the fact that she was making the journey in company with Jack.

They were seated side-by-side, close enough that her wool skirts billowed over one of his legs and her arm inter-mittently brushed against his.

She'd thought sitting beside him would be easier than taking the seat across from him. But just because she couldn't see him without angling her head didn't mean she didn't know he was *there*. His broad-shouldered maleness seemed to fill up the compartment. Even when she wasn't looking at him, she could still smell his cologne. Still hear the steadiness of his every breath.

He was, for the most part, a pleasant companion. At times talkative, amusing her with stories about his family or anecdotes from his time in the army, and at times quiet, gazing out the window with a pensive stare while Bea busied herself writing in her journal.

It was during one of the latter moments, not long after departing the station in Paris at half past eleven in the evening, that Bea tucked her journal away into her traveling valise and asked the question that had been plaguing her since sunset.

"How will we be addressing our sleeping arrangements?"

Jack continued staring out the window as the railway station disappeared into the darkness behind them. He didn't appear to have heard her.

"Jack?" Bea prompted.

"Just making sure they didn't find a way to get back on the train," he said.

Mrs. Rawson and the Farradays had disembarked at the station, but not before making a final visit to Jack and Bea's compartment. Mrs. Rawson had once again encouraged them to join her in Paris. When her entreaties had failed, she and the Farradays had bid Jack and Bea a final adieu.

"Let us not say goodbye," Mrs. Rawson had said. "For we shall meet again."

"We shall," Mrs. Farraday had concurred with a glitter of determination in her eyes. "That much, I vow."

Bea had seen them on the gaslit platform but a few moments ago, Mrs. Farraday looking furious at having been thwarted, Miss Farraday as composed as ever, and Mrs. Rawson wrangling a barking Benjamin with Pearl's assistance.

Jack couldn't have failed to notice them, as intently as he'd been staring out the window.

"That would be impossible, surely," Bea said to him.

"Nothing is impossible where Mrs. Farraday is concerned," he muttered. "Didn't you hear her vowing to see me again? She may even now be clinging to the brake van."

Bea stifled a reflexive grin. She could too easily picture Mrs. Farraday leaping onto the last car of the departing train. "I don't imagine she could hang on for very long. Not with all her petticoats and crinoline."

"That's because you don't know what she's capable of," Jack said grimly. Abandoning the window, he sat back in his seat. "After Paris, she and her daughter will undoubtedly come to Somerset. It won't matter a jot that I'm engaged."

Bea looked at him in the light of the small oil lamp that hung in the corner of their compartment. "But you won't be engaged then, will you? Our engagement ends in Southampton."

Jack met her eyes. "Ah yes. Our amicable breakup."

"Don't say you'd forgotten?"

"On the contrary," Jack said. "I remember everything."

An inexplicable flicker of heat crept up Bea's throat. She ignored it, just as she ignored the scorching memory of their kiss. What else could she do? Nothing could come of it, or of these dratted emotions she'd been feeling.

"Then you must recall what you'd decided to do about this part of the plan," she said in what she hoped was a matter-of-fact manner.

"The sleeping arrangements," Jack replied. "Do you know... I can't say I had a particular plan about those."

The blush stealing into Bea's cheeks burned hotter under his regard. "Mrs. Rawson said there was no sleeper carriage, and that we must sleep sitting up."

"Mrs. Rawson is correct." His mouth curled with faint amusement. "Have you never slept upright before?"

"I have," Bea replied, on her dignity.

But never with a gentleman.

And never with a gentleman she'd kissed but a few days before.

"Are you ready to retire now?" he asked.

"I am," she said.

"You don't need to change into your dressing gown first? Take your hair down? Make your wish on the evening star?"

"I've made my wish, thank you." It had been many hours since sunset. Bea had spent much of that time staring out the window. "And I'm quite all right as I am."

"What else do you require for your comfort?" Jack asked. "Shall I summon the porter to bring you a blanket?"

She was amazed he could be so cavalier about it all. "Do you often sleep with ladies in such conditions?"

His smile reached his eyes. "No," he said. "You'll be the first."

Bea didn't know how to feel about him finding humor in their situation. Not when she couldn't yet tell if it was at her expense. "I'm warm enough without a blanket," she said at length.

"What about a pillow?" he asked. "Or will my shoulder suffice?"

She abandoned any hope of concealing her blushes. It

was many hours yet until they reached Calais. Try as she might, she couldn't pretend indifference for every one of them. For one thing, she was too weary. For another—

"Your shoulder will do nicely," she said.

Jack flashed her a roguish grin. "Not the answer I was expecting, but I'll take it."

Bea removed her bonnet, placing it on the empty seat opposite them. Her pulse was quaking, and her mouth suddenly dry. She hadn't been this close to him since he'd kissed her. But for all the awkwardness of the moment, she really was quite tired.

"If I may?" she asked.

"By all means," Jack replied. "I'm not going anywhere."

Settling herself back in her seat, Bea gingerly rested her head on his shoulder. It was firm beneath her cheek, the soft wool of his overcoat caressing her skin.

Her chest constricted on an unexpected swell of emotion. It had nothing to do with the kiss they'd shared or the butterflies she'd been feeling when she looked at him. It was something else.

Something far more dangerous.

He was so big. So solid.

For the first time in memory, Bea felt safe.

Jack put his arm around her, gathering her into his warmth. "Better?" he asked.

She swallowed the lump that was forming in her throat. How could anything be better? But it was.

Oh, but it was.

"Yes, thank you," she managed.

He turned his face into her hair. "Sleep as long as you need," he said. "I'll wake you when we get to Calais."

Bea wondered how any woman could sleep in such circumstances.

But exhaustion had a way of removing one's inhibitions. Her eyelids grew heavier and, as the train chugged inexorably toward the conclusion of their make-believe romance, she drifted into a boneless slumber in the safety of Jack Beresford's arms.

# Chapter Seventeen

It was half past five in the evening when their steamship from Calais finally reached Southampton. Bea clung to Jack's hand as they navigated the crowds on the docks. She couldn't recall when she'd taken hold of it—or if he'd been the one to take hold of hers. Reaching for each other in moments of chaos had practically become an instinct.

It was a luxury, having someone to act as a protector and guide. Bea wouldn't have thought she'd appreciate it. She was too much an independent person. But the Channel crossing had been treacherous, their steamship rising and falling for hours over the churning waves. Her legs hadn't stopped trembling since they'd reached port.

Jack, meanwhile, appeared entirely unaffected. He was bright-eyed and alert, and not at all unsteady. His weight partially balanced on his cane, he guided her to a less crowded section of the docks, within sight of the cabstand. There they stopped while Jack instructed his batman,

Maberly, to fetch their luggage and to find them suitable transport.

"Yes, sir," Maberly said. "Right away, sir."

When the batman had gone, Jack turned to Bea. "Not long now," he said, still holding her hand.

*Not long until what?* Bea was tempted to ask. Until they hired a carriage? Until he took her to a hotel? Until they said goodbye forever?

It had always been the plan. A plan Bea had willingly agreed to. But during their short time together, what a relief it had been to have someone she could lean on. Someone she could talk to on terms of equality. Someone she could smile with.

But no longer.

Bea forced herself to release her grip on Jack's hand. If they were going to part—

But there was no *if* about it. Their bargain had reached its natural conclusion. It was pointless to cling to him. Trembling knees or no, Bea must once again stand on her own.

Jack swept a concerned look over her. "All right?"

"I don't recall the Channel being that choppy when I left England ten years ago," she said.

"Ten years is a long time. How does it feel to be home again?"

"I don't know," she replied honestly. "I haven't a home here to speak of. Not anymore."

"You will," Jack said. "I'll find you a good situation, Bea. You have my word."

Her heart withered. She didn't know why his promise should be such cold comfort. When she'd left India, a good position was all she'd been hoping for.

But not anymore, it seemed.

All the time she'd spent in Jack's company, pretending to belong *with* him and *to* him, had altered the modest limits of her dreams. She knew now what it was to be looked after, protected, cherished.

None of it had been real, of course. Only a pantomime sufficient to fool the other passengers. Yet in the process, some small part of it had managed to fool Bea too.

"I'm obliged to you," she said. "But a situation isn't the same as a home."

"You'll be settled at least," Jack said. "And safe."

Several ladies and gentlemen pushed past them, wrapped up in overcoats and cloaks, their loud voices carrying on the sea air as they bustled toward the cabstand, or to the carriages that awaited them on the street.

The docks were excessively crowded at this time of evening. Urgency vibrated all about them—a vital, palpable thing. Everyone was coming and going so quickly, so purposefully. Captain Thornhill was among them. Bea saw him in the distance, making his way toward two gentlemen who were striding to greet him. One was a slim, bespectacled fellow, and the other a blond giant of a man in a brown cloth coat. The giant came forward to embrace the captain while the man in the spectacles looked on with a smile.

Jack followed Bea's gaze. "Thornhill spoke truly, then," he mused. "He did have someone coming to meet him."

"His family, perhaps," Bea suggested, though none of the men bore any resemblance to each other.

"Not his family. His attorney. A friend of his, I gather, along with the other fellow." Jack gave a satisfied nod. "They'll look after him."

"You sound relieved."

"I am," he said. "It's tedious feeling responsible for everyone. I've had the devil of a time shedding the impulse after leaving the army." His eyes glinted with a flash of humor. "For a while there, I feared I'd have to issue the man an invitation to join my family in Somerset. They wouldn't have thanked me for it, nor would Thornhill. Thank heaven he has people of his own."

Bea's eyes fell to her hands. It seemed that everyone had a home to return to, and friends and family to meet. Even someone as cross and curmudgeonly as Captain Thornhill.

It made her predicament that much lonelier.

She smoothed her gloves with restless fingers as the last of the steamship passengers hurried by. Time was ticking past more rapidly than she wished it to, bringing the two of them ever closer to their inevitable goodbyes.

There was no point pretending it was otherwise.

Lifting her chin, Bea forced her gaze back to his. "Is this where we have our amicable breakup?"

Jack gave her a puzzled frown. "Here on the docks?"

"We can't very well have it in a hotel room," she said. "Indeed, I don't think you should accompany me to the hotel at all."

"You'd prefer a separate carriage?" His brow furrowed. "I suppose it makes sense. Though I can't be at ease until I see that your lodgings are respectable."

"I'm the best judge of that. I've been managing my own affairs for a long while now. And it wouldn't do for us to show up together at a hotel, even in separate carriages. I can't afford any talk."

His mouth quirked. "You're not going to be difficult, are you?"

"I'm not being difficult. I'm being realistic. We had a plan and we must stick to it, for both of our sakes."

"I mean to. But even you must admit that things haven't gone exactly as we intended."

Bea folded her arms, thinking of the shawl he'd given her. Thinking of their kiss, and all the small moments that had followed in its aftermath. The way he readily took her hand. The way he'd put his arm around her as she'd slept against his shoulder on the overnight train to Calais.

She swallowed the lump that was forming in her throat. "I don't know what you mean."

The amused expression in his eyes softened. "Don't you, Bea?"

"Unless you're referencing what happened that night on the deck—"

"Among other things."

Her stomach quivered with the threat of butterflies. She ignored the tremulous sensation as best she could. "That was days ago."

"Five days, to be precise. I don't take it lightly."

"Nor do I. Which is nothing to the point. Unless..."

His attention sharpened. "Unless what?"

Bea summoned her courage. If this was the last time she was to see him, she may as well leave all her cards on the table. She'd never get another chance. She took a deep breath. "Unless you mean to make your proposal in earnest," she said.

Jack froze, staring at her. The color drained from his face, leaving him peculiarly pale beneath his tan.

It was answer enough.

The unspoken rejection travelled through her, putting

an end to her butterflies and her blushes. There were no more flutterings, no more warmth, only a growing coldness at her core.

This, then, was reality. The way Jack truly felt about her. She wasn't entirely surprised by it. Even so...

*Good lord.* Did he have to look so horrified by the prospect of her being his real fiancée instead of his false one?

"Obviously you don't," she said tersely. "As I'm well aware. I was merely attempting to make a point. You needn't gawp at me in horror as though you'd just seen a ghost."

Jack's stark gaze found hers. She realized then, much to her astonishment, that he hadn't been looking at her at all. Rather, he'd been staring at something over her shoulder. "Not a ghost," he said. "My oldest brother."

---

JACK SWALLOWED HARD AS HIS EYES ONCE AGAIN found James on the opposite end of the dock. It was undoubtedly him. There was no mistaking that towering height, that golden Beresford hair, and that glacial expression, unthawed by the passage of time.

It had been more than three years since Jack's last visit home, but James looked no different now than he had then. Clad in an impeccably cut black three-piece suit, he stood beside his wife, Hannah. She was an undisputed beauty, with a mass of upswept dark auburn hair and a face distinguished by the gentleness of its expression.

*Bloody blasted hell.*

"How the devil did they know—" Jack began.

But in that exact moment James's icy gaze found his.

Jack's stomach sank. There would be no extricating himself now. He forced himself to smile at his brother.

James returned the wordless greeting with a slight smile of his own.

"Your oldest brother?" Bea repeated in dismay. "The Viscount St. Clare?"

"That's the one," Jack said.

"Shall I away?" she asked. "I can go straight to the hotel or—"

"It's too late for that," Jack said.

James was already making his way toward them, with Hannah on his arm. The crowd seemed to part for him, as though in tacit acknowledgment of the authority he wielded, both as heir to the earldom and as a gentleman to be reckoned with in his own right.

"The hero returns," James said as he and his wife approached. They came to a halt in front of Jack and Bea. "And with a cane, no less."

"A temporary necessity after my surgery," Jack replied.

James looked Jack over with a rare show of brotherly concern. "It was a success?"

"So, I'm told," Jack said. "How did you know—"

"That you'd be arriving today?" Hannah embraced Jack. "We received a wire yesterday informing us of your travel plans—and of your engagement." Withdrawing from him, she turned to Bea with a warm smile. "You must be Miss Layton."

To her credit, Bea didn't bat an eye. Neither did she speak.

Jack maintained his smile through sheer strength of will. "Someone has spoiled my surprise."

"Then it's true?" James's attention settled on Bea.

Bea stood ramrod straight under his regard. Steeling herself, very probably. This was, after all, the moment Jack must disabuse his relations of their misapprehension. He must tell them either that Bea was not in fact his fiancé, or that she had been so during the voyage, but was no longer. Either way, their relationship would shortly be severed. Bea would go to her hotel and Jack would go with his family, and that would be an end to it.

Simple enough.

But when Jack opened his mouth to do so, the words wouldn't come.

At least, not *those* words.

"Bea, may I present my brother James, Lord St. Clare, and his wife Hannah, Lady St. Clare," he heard himself say. "James, Hannah, this is Miss Beatrice Layton, my fiancée."

Hannah beamed. "Then, it *is* true." She extended her gloved hands to Bea. "How pleased I am to meet you, Miss Layton."

Bea hesitated for a fraction of a second before taking Hannah's hands in return. "And I you, my lady."

"Hannah, please," Hannah said. "And may I call you Beatrice? Or do you prefer Bea?"

"Either will suffice," Bea said.

James offered Bea a bow. "Miss Layton."

Bea inclined her head to him. "My lord."

Before either of them could utter another word, Maberly materialized with Jack's and Bea's luggage on a hand cart. He wasn't unacquainted with Jack's family, having accompanied Jack home on leave multiple times during his years serving as Jack's batman.

"Your luggage, Colonel Beresford," he said, perspiration dotting his brow. "And Miss Layton's. Where shall I—"

"You may load it onto my carriage, Maberly," James said. "It's by the cab stand. My footman will assist you."

"Yes, my lord." Maberly bobbed his head before obediently haring off with the bags.

Jack's fingers tightened on the handle of his cane. "Who sent the wire?" he asked his brother.

"A Mrs. Rawson," James said. "She claims an acquaintance with me."

"Mrs. Rawson, of course." Jack might have known.

"She was concerned about you traveling home in comfort," James said. "And about Miss Layton being properly chaperoned."

"Not to worry on either count," Hannah said. "We have brought our traveling coach. And I am here to ensure Miss Layton isn't without female companionship." She addressed Bea. "You must be dreadfully tired after traveling all through the night."

"I am," Bea admitted. "But you needn't put yourself to any trouble on my account."

"Nonsense." Hannah slipped her arm through Bea's. "You are soon to be my sister-in-law. You must allow me to take care of you."

Jack exchanged a weighted glance with Bea as Hannah drew her toward the waiting carriage. The single look seemed to contain an entire conversation.

*"Why on earth didn't you tell them the truth?"* she asked with her eyes.

*"It's complicated,"* he answered back silently. *"My brother wouldn't understand."*

*"What about our amicable breakup?"*

*"Later."*

*"And my reference?"*

*"You'll have your reference. I gave you my word and I mean to keep it. I just require a bit of time."*

Jack had never communicated so much with another person in his life. Not without words. Not in a single scorching look.

But things with Bea had always been different, hadn't they? She hadn't chased him. Hadn't wanted him. She had, he was fairly certain, at one time thought he might be insane.

Given their current predicament, Jack wouldn't be at all surprised if she was reconsidering that diagnosis.

"Where did you meet her?" James asked.

Jack turned his attention to his brother. Despite all these years, James still had the ability to make him feel like a feckless boy of eighteen. "On the voyage home from India."

"Rather hasty on your part."

"Not at all. We were many weeks at sea."

"Precisely my point," James said. "It's hardly enough time to get to know a person. Not sufficient for marriage."

"No?"

"And she's not altogether your type, is she?"

Jack fixed his brother with a warning glare. "What is my type, James?"

James returned Jack's gaze, undaunted. "You used to prefer them rather less quiet in their allurements."

*Quiet?*

Jack was tempted to laugh.

Beatrice Layton was anything but quiet.

She walked ahead of them, arm and arm with Hannah, her spine straight and her slim shoulders squared—unbent, unbroken—despite everything life had thrown at her. Despite what *Jack* had thrown at her.

Admiration rose in his breast. It was coupled with an unmistakable warmth.

"Perhaps I've grown up," he said.

## Chapter Eighteen

It was dark by the time Lord and Lady St. Clare's lavish traveling coach entered the gates of their vast Somerset estate. Beasley Park, it was called. At one time the childhood home of their mother, it was now the primary residence of the viscount and his family.

Bea had learned much about its history during the long drive to Somerset. Lady St. Clare—or rather, Hannah—had told Bea all. She was a kindly lady, with a gentle aspect and a solicitous manner.

Unlike her husband.

In comparison to the warmth of his wife, Lord St. Clare might have been carved from a block of ice. He said little during the journey, and smiled even less. His expression was closed off. Reflective. As though he were attempting to solve a vexing puzzle. When he wasn't looking at Jack, he was looking at Bea, the vaguest suggestion of a frown etching his brow.

Bea felt the unhappy weight of his scrutiny too many

times to count during their journey. It was an unpleasant reminder of the deception she and Jack were perpetrating.

A deception that had been meant to end hours ago on the Southampton docks.

Bea dared another glance at Jack from beneath her lashes as the coach came to a crunching halt on the estate's graveled drive. He was on the velvet upholstered seat across from her, his hardened countenance nearly as unreadable as that of his older brother.

His leg was paining him, Bea suspected. And he was angry at having his plans thwarted by his family. Not to mention the fact that, but a few seconds before his brother had appeared on the docks, she'd had the temerity to suggest the ludicrous possibility that they might turn their fake engagement into a real one.

Bea inwardly winced to recall it.

If only she could have a moment to speak with Jack alone, she was certain the two of them could sort everything out. And they *must* sort things out, and soon, before the situation got any worse.

A footman opened the carriage door. Lord St. Clare descended first so that he could hand his wife down. Jack climbed out after her, ignoring his brother's offer of help.

A retinue of liveried servants emerged from the house under the command of a stately gentleman who appeared to be the butler. "The bags, Alfred," he was saying. "And you, Duncan, see to that trunk."

Amid all this activity, Jack turned and extended his hand to Bea.

Bea took it gratefully, allowing him to assist her down from the carriage. "Jack," she said under her breath. "What are we going to do?"

"I'm trying to think of something," he muttered back.

Bea gripped tight to his hand. "Think faster."

In that same moment, four children of various sizes hurtled from the house, bounding down the torchlit steps and across the drive. There were two boys in short pants and two girls in pinafores and hair ribbons. None appeared to be any older than twelve, and the smallest among them—an auburn-haired little imp—might have been as young as six.

Three large dogs galloped along with them; a wolfhound, and two scruffy coated mongrels of dubious origin. Their jubilant barks intermingled with the children's equally excited shouts and squeals.

Hannah's expression softened. "Oh goodness. I told the children they weren't to wait up for us."

"Uncle Jack!" the oldest boy called. He was the first to reach them, along with the still barking wolfhound. His face was wreathed in smiles. "Did you get my letter?"

Jack smiled broadly in return. Dropping Bea's hand, he stepped forward to embrace the lad with one arm. "Of course I did, and responded to it too."

"I haven't received any reply yet," the boy said.

"I'm not surprised," Jack told him. "I've likely beat it here."

The second oldest boy was close on the first boy's heels. The other two dogs danced around him, big bodies wiggling and tails wagging, nearly causing the child to lose his balance. "What about my letter, Uncle Jack? I sent you the watercolors I did on our holiday in Derbyshire. The ones of the peaks."

"I hung them in my quarters," Jack said, hugging the boy in turn. "And wished like the devil I could have been there with you."

"Uncle Jack!" the little girls cried in unison. They clutched at Jack's trouser legs and pulled at his coat, surrounding him in company with their brothers and the barking dogs. "Uncle Jack! What did you bring us?"

"Greedy as ever," Jack teased. He bent to kiss the girls. "I thought you'd grown out of surprise gifts?" He tugged the youngest one's plaits. "Hadn't you Charlotte? Or is that Agatha I'm thinking of?"

"Not me," the older girl replied.

"Nor me," the littlest one said. "Did you bring me a puppy? Or a kitten?"

"Don't be stupid," the younger boy chided. "He can't put puppies and kittens in his traveling trunks."

"Mind how you speak to your sister," Lord St. Clare said to his son.

"Sorry, Charlotte," the boy uttered promptly. "But really, Papa," he added with a long-suffering look at his father. "Puppies and kittens? As if we don't have enough already."

"Come, my dears." Hannah urged the girls away from Jack. "Don't overwhelm your uncle."

"And mind his leg," Lord St. Clare warned the oldest boy. "That cane isn't a toy."

Bea hung behind Jack in the shadow of the coach as the dogs sniffed at her skirts. She would have shrunk back still further if Jack hadn't extended his hand to her again. The children peered at her as she took it. There was no malice in their expressions, only curiosity.

"Who is that lady, Uncle Jack?" the older of the girls asked.

"Is that your new wife?" the littlest wondered.

"Not his wife," the older boy said. "His *betrothed*."

"This is Miss Layton," Jack informed them. He drew Bea forward to stand at his side. "Bea, these are my rapscallion nieces and nephews. That's Nicholas, his younger brother, Arthur, and their sisters, Agatha and Charlotte. Scapegraces all, and markedly bigger than when I last saw them. Especially you, Nick. You look more like your father by the year."

"I'm pleased to make your acquaintances," Bea said. "Your uncle has spoken of you often."

The four children continued to gape at her until their father sent them a stern look. They responded in a flash, sketching formal bows and dropping dainty curtsies, as though they were miniature lords and ladies greeting a dignitary at court. "Miss Layton," they said in unison.

Bea smiled in spite of herself. She had been too much in company with the Dimsdales. She'd almost forgotten how endearing children could be. And these ones *were* endearing, with their eager faces, their innocent exuberance, and their pack of raucous dogs.

"Let us go in," Hannah said. She encouraged the dogs and children to precede them before turning her attention to Bea. "You must be longing for your bed."

"I am, rather," Bea confessed.

"Our housekeeper has made up your rooms for you." Hannah set a hand on Bea's back, guiding her inside. "I shall take you to yours myself."

Bea relinquished Jack's hand, allowing Hannah to escort her up the stone steps and into the house's marble entry hall. There, in the light of a blazing chandelier, they were met by a helpful footman who divested them of their hats, bonnets, coats, and gloves. Even more footmen carried in their trunks and cases, while a kindly looking woman in a ruffled apron appeared at the top of the stairs to take the children back to the nursery.

"What about our presents?" Charlotte asked Jack.

Jack had entered the hall with Lord St. Clare only a few seconds behind Bea and Hannah. "Tomorrow," he promised.

"At breakfast," Nicholas insisted. "First thing."

"I will come and wake you," Arthur said.

Jack chuckled. "I shall be sure to lock my chamber door."

"Which trunk holds our presents?" Agatha asked. "We could find them ourselves and—"

"That's enough, my loves," Hannah said to the children. "Your uncle and Miss Layton have been traveling for weeks. You must give them a chance to rest. Mrs. Lovell? If you please?"

"Come, children," Mrs. Lovell said. "Do as you're told. There's time enough for all that in the morning."

The children grudgingly mounted the stairs to join their nanny. The dogs ran up the steps with them amid calls of "Goodnight!" and "Sleep well!" and "Don't forget, Uncle Jack!"

Lord St. Clare exchanged a private glance with his wife. "We'll be fortunate if they sleep at all."

"Poor dears," Hannah said. "They've been so dreadfully excited." She turned to Jack and Bea. "Are either of you desirous of dinner? Cook suggested a cold collation in the dining room, but given the hour, I thought you might prefer trays in your bedchambers."

"An excellent idea," Jack said.

"Shall we have a glass of brandy before you retire?" Lord St. Clare asked Jack.

Jack's expression sobered. "If you insist."

Hannah smiled. "We shall bid you goodnight, then."

Jack looked at Bea. Bea thought she detected a glimmer of apology in his eyes.

And well he should apologize.

It was one thing to lie to the Mrs. Rawsons and Mrs. Farradays of the world. It was quite another to lie to Jack's family. A family who obviously adored him, and who he loved deeply in return.

Every moment that passed without telling them the truth only served to exacerbate Jack and Bea's crime.

Bea wanted no part of it. Not when Hannah was so lovely and gracious and the children were so charming. But what could Bea do? It wasn't up to her to betray their secret. Only Jack could do that.

Her eyes followed him as he and his brother departed together down the candlelit corridor.

Hannah's smile dimmed. "They'll be going to the library," she said. "To converse over a glass of something strong. It's best we give them a moment."

Bea could only imagine what the conversation would entail. No doubt Lord St. Clare would be interrogating Jack about his sudden engagement.

As Hannah showed Bea up the grand, curving staircase to a prettily appointed upstairs bedroom, Bea realized that her hostess had similar ideas.

"We were excessively surprised to receive Mrs. Rawson's message yesterday," Hannah said, closing the door behind them. She turned up the glass oil lamp that burned on a nearby table, casting the room in a soft halo of light. "We'd long resigned ourselves to Jack ending his days as a bachelor."

Bea cast a distracted glance around the bedchamber. It was generously sized, decorated in soft florals and pale Aubusson, with a chintz-curtained four-poster bed at its center. An exceedingly comfortable space, that had little in common with the small, sparsely furnished rooms she'd inhabited during her many years as a governess.

"Mrs. Rawson should not have shared the news before we'd had a chance to do so ourselves," Bea said.

"No, she shouldn't have," Hannah agreed. "Though I'm grateful that she did, given your situation."

Bea's brows lifted. "My situation?"

"Arriving in England with Jack, without a maid or a chaperone," Hannah said. Her understanding expression robbed her words of any hint of censure. "What did you plan to do?"

"I intended to stay at a hotel," Bea said.

"Until Jack could speak with us, presumably." Wandering to the bed, Hannah gave an absent tug on the coverlet, straightening its edge. "In that case, I'm glad Mrs. Rawson informed us of your engagement. We'd far rather you stay at Beasley Park than put up at a lonely hotel."

"It would have been no hardship," Bea said. "I'm accustomed to fending for myself."

"Haven't you any family?" Hannah asked.

Bea saw no reason to sugarcoat the matter. "Both of my parents are dead."

Hannah's eyes softened with sympathy. "I'm very sorry to hear it."

"It was a long time ago. Nearly ten years."

"May I ask who they were?"

"No one of importance," Bea said. "Except to me." She hesitated before elaborating, "They were neither rich, nor titled, but my father was a gentleman. He left enough for me to obtain my schooling, so that I might have a secure position in life."

Hannah looked at her in question.

"After losing them, I was sent to a school where I was trained to be a governess," Bea said.

"I see," Hannah murmured.

"I've been in India nearly ten years altogether. I've spent the whole of it working. It's nothing I'm ashamed of."

"Nor why should you be?" Hannah crossed to the window. She smoothed one of the curtains. "How did you and Jack—?"

"On the ship sailing out of Alexandria," Bea answered before Hannah could finish her question. "I was in a difficult predicament with my employers, and Jack was attempting to avoid certain of the passengers."

Hannah's mouth ticked up at one corner. "*Lady* passengers?"

"Indeed."

"Dear Jack," Hannah said with a laugh. "Some things never change." She paused, explaining, "He's been quite sought after in his time."

"Ruthlessly sought after, apparently," Bea said. "Or so he's told me."

Hannah's smile turned quizzical. "Has he?"

"We are used to speaking frankly with each other."

"I didn't know Jack *could* speak frankly. He's more likely to jest." Hannah finished arranging the curtain. She turned back to Bea. "What a shock it was to everyone when he decided to join the army."

Bea was curious in spite of herself. "Why so?" she asked.

"Don't younger sons of the nobility often purchase a commission?"

"Second sons sometimes do. Third sons are generally for the church." Hannah smiled again. "An even less suitable position for someone of Jack's temperament."

"I'd have said he was well suited for the army."

"Would you? I daresay you're right. Though it's such a serious profession. And he needn't have taken it up. He has ample means at his disposal, and a handsome estate of his own now. Not but that he's had more than a few weeks at a time to live in it. He only visits Somerset when he's on leave, and sometimes not even then. The children have met him but a handful of times."

"Only that?" Bea was surprised. "But they seem to adore him."

"Oh, they do," Hannah said. "Jack has a way with children. My husband would say it's because Jack is still a bit of a child himself. He's always had an appreciation for larking about. I'm pleased to see that hasn't changed, despite his elevation in rank."

Bea instantly thought of that night on the deck of the Pera when Jack had proposed their fake engagement.

"I'm far too old for such a childish prank," she'd told him.

"I'm not," Jack had replied promptly. "Not if it serves."

"He has that knack, you know," Hannah said. "To dazzle in small doses. Which is rather convenient, since a little of himself is all he's usually disposed to share before he's off again."

Bea frowned. Was that a warning? It was difficult to tell. "He won't be off this time," she said.

"No, indeed," Hannah agreed. "Not now he has you."

# Chapter Nineteen

James poured Jack a glass of brandy and motioned him to one of the chairs in front of the library hearth. A dwindling fire crackled in the fireplace, casting shadows over the dark, bookcase-lined walls and the red-and-gold carpeted floor. James lit a branch of candles on the mantlepiece before taking a seat himself. He didn't beat about the bush.

"Who is she?" he asked.

Jack had been preparing himself for the question ever since he'd locked eyes with his brother on the docks. "My fiancée," he answered.

"You know what I mean."

"I do," Jack said. "And my answer should be enough."

"Under normal circumstances."

Jack took a grudging drink. The brandy burned his throat as he swallowed. "These are abnormal?"

"Where you're concerned, yes. This all seems out of character." James's gaze was as incisive as ever. "Unless, it's *in* character."

Jack didn't flinch. Naturally James suspected there was something more going on than a simple engagement. He knew Jack. Knew that he'd once had a fondness for high-stakes schemes. That didn't mean Jack was going to admit to anything.

"Perhaps you don't know my character as well as you think you do," he said.

"I know you weren't in the market for a wife."

"I wasn't. But things change. People change. I'm not a lad anymore."

James didn't reply straightaway. He let the silence stretch between them for several tension-filled seconds. "Is there something you're not telling me?" he inquired at last.

"Is there something *you're* not telling *me*?" Jack asked in return.

James raised his glass to his lips. "Such as?"

Jack studied his brother's face in the firelight. Once, his lack of expression might have stymied Jack, but no longer. "Something else Mrs. Rawson said in her wire, perhaps?"

"Ah. That." Setting aside his glass, James stood and went to his desk. He opened one of the drawers, retrieving a telegram from within. He handed it to Jack. "It wasn't Mrs. Rawson."

Jack examined the telegram with a frown. It had been sent anonymously, but the office of origin was plainly marked. It had come from the railway station in Marseilles.

COLONEL BERESFORD ENTRAPPED BY ADVEN-TURESS. HONOR PREVENTS HIM EXTRI-CATING HIMSELF. IMMEDIATE ASSISTANCE REQUIRED.

Jack lowered the telegram, outrage giving way to cold fury. "When did you get this?"

"Yesterday. It arrived at the same time as the telegram from Mrs. Rawson." James returned to his seat. "Any idea who it might be from?"

"A woman by the name of Mrs. Farraday."

"Dare I ask?"

"She's a lady with a marriageable daughter who has dogged my steps for more than a year." Jack crumpled the telegram in his fist. "Who else knows about this?"

"No one."

"Not Hannah?"

James retrieved his drink. "Not yet."

"Not ever," Jack said. "I won't have this rubbish being bandied about where Bea might hear of it. And I won't have it influencing any of you in your opinions about her."

"'Entrapped by an adventuress,'" James murmured. "Rather specific."

"It's scurrilous nonsense."

"With no shred of truth to it?"

"No," Jack said. "Bea's no adventuress. She's a governess. Or rather, she was one before we became engaged."

"I see."

Jack's brows lowered. "You're not seriously objecting to her former profession?"

James shrugged. "I merely find it interesting, given the nature of that second telegram."

"It's predictable is what it is," Jack said. "Mrs. Farraday will stop at nothing. She's a widow, with dwindling prospects. Her daughter is currency to her."

"Has she reason to—"

"No." Jack made a disparaging sound as he threw the telegram into the fire. It immediately caught flame. "I've never treated either of them with anything more than basic courtesy. As for my honor—it's that she was banking on as a means of trapping me into marrying her daughter. It didn't work. Largely thanks to Bea."

James looked at Jack with increased attention.

"And Bea isn't after my fortune, by the way," Jack added. "Or the distinction of the Beresford name. When she met me, she didn't even know who I was. I was traveling incognito."

"This becomes more interesting by the minute," James said. "Traveling incognito? Pursued by one lady and now engaged to another? Is there anything else I should know about? Any other pursuers?"

Jack downed another swallow of his brandy. "You may well be amused. You've been married so long, you've forgotten what it's like to be chased."

"I haven't forgotten. The difference is, my pursuers knew they hadn't a chance with me. While yours have always believed you would imminently propose."

"That's because I have a pulse," Jack retorted. "And because I'm civil. Perhaps if I'd treated them with icy disdain—"

"Perhaps you should have done, rather than giving them false hope." James fell quiet for a moment. "Miss Layton did *not* pursue you, I take it."

Jack huffed. "Not at all. She's not that kind of girl."

"What kind is she?"

"The kind that's used to soldiering alone," Jack said. He heaved a sigh. "I wish you hadn't met us at the docks. I fear it's all going to be too much for her. You, and Hannah, and the children."

"She'd have had to meet us eventually."

Jack averted his gaze from his brother's. No, Bea wouldn't have had to meet them. Had Jack and Bea parted on the docks as they'd planned, none of the Beresfords would ever have known her at all.

The prospect provoked a heavy weight in Jack's chest. He didn't want to think of never seeing Bea again. Never smiling with her. Never kissing her.

"Wouldn't she?" James asked.

Jack glanced back at his brother. He seemed to have lost track of their conversation. "Sorry," he said. "I drifted off."

"Is it your leg?"

"It's lack of sleep. I was awake the whole way through France, and during the Channel crossing. It's finally caught up with me."

"Well," James said. "I won't keep you from your bed."

"I'm obliged to you." Jack gripped his cane, moving to rise.

James remained in his chair. "There is, however, one other matter I must bring to your attention."

Jack stilled. "If it's another anonymous telegram, I won't be held responsible for my actions."

"It's not another telegram."

"Then can it wait?"

James gestured for Jack to resume his seat. "I'm afraid it can't."

# Chapter Twenty

Bea was awakened the next morning before sunrise, not by the efforts of the maid her hostess had lent her the previous evening, but by a soft and rather insistent knock on her chamber door. She had an immediate sense who it might be. Answering the surreptitious summons a moment later, clad in her dressing gown, with her hair still in its nighttime plait, her feminine intuition was proved right.

"Jack," she whispered. "What are you doing here?"

He stood in the darkened hall, leaning heavily on his cane. He was dressed for the out of doors in a wool topcoat and trousers. "We need to talk," he said quietly.

"We absolutely do," she agreed. "But not, I should think, in my bedroom."

"Naturally not in your bedroom. Not in the hall either. How soon can you be dressed?"

"What did you have in mind?"

"There's a secluded place along the banks of a stream

that runs through the grounds. It's far enough away from the house that we won't be disturbed."

Bea nodded solemnly. "Give me five minutes."

Closing the door, she hurried to wash and dress. It took longer than she'd anticipated, owing to difficulties finding a suitably warm dress and stockings in the hodgepodge of packing cases the footmen had brought up last night. Once discovered, she hastily put them on, and equally hastily brushed out her plait, twisting her hair back into a loose chignon at her nape. Collecting the cashmere shawl Jack had given her, she at last exited her room.

Jack was leaning against the wall outside her door. He straightened when he saw her. "Ready?"

"Ready."

"It's this way," he said.

Wrapping her shawl around her shoulders, Bea silently followed him along the corridor and down the curving staircase. Rather than crossing the marble entry hall to the house's front doors, Jack led her down another flight of stairs to the kitchens.

Unlike the rest of the house, the kitchens were already lit, with servants bustling about, and an aged, aproned cook standing over an enormous iron stove, presiding over an array of steaming pots and kettles.

Jack winked at the old woman as they passed through, provoking her into a smile. "She's been here since I was a lad," he said to Bea as he opened the back door for her.

Bea preceded him outside, where dawn was breaking rapidly over the verdant, mist-covered landscape. A chill wind nipped at her face and ruffled her hair. "Is this where you grew up?" she asked.

Jack closed the door after them. "In large part." He offered Bea his arm. "My parents split their time between Beasley Park and Worth House, our family seat in Hertfordshire. But they far preferred it here. This is where my mother was born, and where she met my father as a girl. It's where they fell in love."

Bea slipped her hand through Jack's arm. As they left the kitchen yard, making their way over the sloping lawn toward a stand of trees in the distance, she couldn't be entirely sure whether she was relying on him for support or he was relying on her.

It occurred to her that, perhaps, it was mutual. Each of them needing the other an equal amount to get where they were going. To keep from falling or losing their way.

The thought brought Bea some small comfort. Especially now, when Jack's family, and anyone else she and Jack met, might reasonably view their arrangement as being appallingly one-sided.

Sunlight streaked through the branches ahead of them, burning away the morning fog and lighting their way through the trees. Bea heard the stream before she saw it— the melodic trickle of softly rippling water. And then it was there, before them, framed by gently sloping banks covered in a profusion of blue wildflowers.

They were forget-me-nots, Bea realized. As dazzling a display of them as she'd ever seen in her life. "How beautiful," she whispered.

"It always is at this time of year," Jack said. He guided her carefully down the bank, finding purchase with his cane.

"Are you sure you're able—"

"I'm not a complete invalid."

She gripped his arm. "I wasn't implying that you were. Only that, if you fell—"

"I won't," he said. "Anyway, we're nearly there. Do you see that fallen tree?"

Bea followed his gaze to an old, dried-out trunk at the edge of the water. It was hardly a park bench, but it would do. Jack escorted her to it. He remained standing until she seated herself. Only then did he join her.

"Your sister-in-law's maid will be dismayed not to find me in my room when she comes to wake me," Bea remarked.

"I doubt it," Jack said. "My family has so far seemed to predict my every move."

Her eyes jerked to his in swift alarm. "Don't say they've already guessed that our engagement is a false one?"

"No. Not exactly." Jack pushed his fingers through his hair. The thick blond strands shone like golden wheat in the newly risen sun. "But my brother doesn't entirely believe it's real either."

Bea waited for him to explain, her stomach tense.

"I have a reputation, you see." He paused. "*Had* a reputation."

"For larking about?"

His brows notched. "Someone's already told you?"

"Mrs. Rawson mentioned it on the Pera," Bea reminded him. "And Hannah referenced it last night."

Jack frowned. "Yes, well... It isn't true any longer." He paused, adding, "And they were never *larks*. I merely enjoyed risks. Dares, contests, and the like. My little sister is the same. We used to set challenges for each other when we were younger, much to James's disapproval. He was constantly after me to behave in a more dignified manner. Since joining the army, I like to think I have. I've distinguished myself. Moved through the ranks. Proved that

James is wrong. That I'm not a reckless idiot, incapable of exercising sound judgment."

"I see," Bea murmured.

"Do you?" Jack asked. "Do you really, Bea?"

"When he met us on the docks yesterday, you were afraid you'd be proving him right."

"I would have been, had I told him that you and I were no longer engaged. Or worse, that we'd never been engaged in the first place. That's why I said what I said. I'm sorry I didn't consult with you first. I know it wasn't part of our agreement. But—"

"I don't want to lie to your family, Jack,"

"I know," he said. "Nor do I."

A breeze drifted over the banks, making the wildflowers quiver. Bea gazed at them for a long moment, her spirits sinking as low as they'd ever been. It wasn't right to be here with Jack, in a place so beautiful and remote, so exceedingly romantic, discussing something as bleak as their imminent parting.

But one had to face facts.

"What if I left now?" she suggested. "Quiet-like, without any fuss. Just slip away to the hotel and...when I'm gone...you could simply tell them the truth?"

Jack's ice-gray eyes were unusually grave. "Face James and Hannah on my own, you mean?"

A flicker of guilt took Bea unaware. She was abandoning him. It was cowardly. Disloyal.

Yet, it was his lie that had brought them here, not hers. She'd been ready to walk away at the docks. Any other woman in her position would do the same. It wasn't a matter of loyalty. It was a question of self-preservation.

"Yes," she replied.

"But it won't just be them any longer," Jack said. "That's what I came to tell you this morning. When James and I spoke last night, he informed me that my other relations are expected today. My brother, Ivo, and his wife, Meg. My sister, Kate, and her husband, Charles. All of their children. Not to mention my parents, who will be arriving by Saturday. It's to be something of a family party."

The blood left Bea's face. She recalled everything Mrs. Rawson and the Farradays had told her about the Beresfords. About their wealth and pedigree. About their fashionableness and extraordinary good looks. It was one thing to meet Jack's oldest brother and his wife, but to confront the family entire? The mere prospect of it was enough to send a chill down Bea's spine.

"It was Hannah's idea, apparently," Jack said grimly. "Hers and Meg's, sparked by that dratted wire Mrs. Rawson sent them. They've already got it planned. A week-long celebration to welcome home the injured hero, culminating in a ball, with all the village in attendance." He paused. "There's only one problem."

Bea immediately thought of his injury. "You can't dance?"

Jack's mouth twisted. "I'm not a hero."

# Chapter Twenty-One

Bea stared at him. Of all the replies she'd been expecting, it hadn't been *that*. "I thought you were going to say it was your leg."

"Two problems, then," Jack acknowledged. "Likely more if I took the time to identify them."

Bea studied his face, striving to understand. He looked so closed off. So hard and alone. It wasn't like Jack. Not the Jack she had come to know.

"I don't know why you'd say such a thing in the first place," she said. "To claim you aren't a hero? What nonsense." A thought occurred to her. "It's not... That is, it isn't because of *how* you were injured, is it?"

"It is," he admitted.

Her lips thinned in reproof. "Just because your horse fell on you in battle doesn't make your sacrifice any less heroic. You were still fighting for Queen and country, weren't you? And all injuries in service to the Crown are—"

Jack cut her off. "That's not what happened."

Bea stilled. "But you said—"

"I said my horse fell on me during a skirmish."

"During a battle, I thought. At..." Her brows knit. What had he called it? "Mohammerah?"

He gave a terse nod.

"Yet, that's not the whole of it," she concluded. "You're saying there was more."

"There was. But... It's not anything I can talk about."

"Why not?" She sunk her voice. "Is it a secret?"

"Something like that."

Bea could think of no better place to confide one than here beside the stream in the shelter of trees, with forget-me-nots blanketing the sloping banks around them. The secluded spot was a secret in itself. No one else seemed to exist here but her and Jack. Just the two of them on the ancient fallen tree, side-by-side, just as they'd been in their railway compartment on their journey from Marseilles.

A scrap of birdsong broke the silence—a sweet, melodic sound. It was carried away on the breeze. Only the sound of the rippling water remained.

"You're the one who brought it up," Bea pointed out.

"I often find myself telling you far more than I should," Jack said. "Why is that, do you suppose?" His voice took on a sardonic edge. "Is it because you're so extraordinarily sympathetic?"

Bea suppressed a huff of amusement. "I'm not *un*sympathetic."

"Pragmatic, I should have said. Unless someone wrongs you one too many times. Or unless they wrong one of your friends. In which case, all bets are off."

Amusement fading, Bea regarded him with unusual solemnity. They'd been through so much together in so short a time. All those hours on the Pera, on the train across

France, and on the steamer over the Channel. All those miles traveled, shoulder-to-shoulder and hand-in-hand.

"I count *you* as a friend," she said.

A rare glimmer of vulnerability flickered at the back of Jack's gaze. "Do you, Bea?"

"I do," she said. "Which is why I won't interrogate you on the subject of your last battle, or skirmish, or whatever you'd like to call it. I've no wish for you to put your honor at risk revealing the clandestine operations of the British government."

A bitter smile edged Jack's mouth. "It's not a military secret," he said. "Merely a shameful one."

Her brows lifted in question. But she didn't press him. She merely waited.

Jack set his hand on the curved handle of his cane. He looked at it for several weighted seconds before he spoke. "The fighting at Mohammerah lasted less than a week," he said at last. "Our forces ultimately prevailed, but on the final night, when we took the city, two of our men fired on us as we were chasing down the retreating Persian army."

Bea's eyes went wide. "Your own men?"

"It was later determined to be an accident."

"But how—?"

"It was dark and all was in chaos," Jack said. His attention remained on his cane. "My horse went down and me along with him. It broke my leg. Partially crushed it. I must have fainted, for when I next opened my eyes, I was in a field hospital and some boy-child of a surgeon was doing his best for me. Regrettably, his best wasn't very good. Which was all of a piece with the whole wretched affair. When I think of it..."

Bea waited for him to finish his thought, but he did not.

"Why would you call it shameful?" she asked when the silence between them had stretched too long for her comfort.

"What else to call it? I was fired at by my own men. Injured by my own horse. And everything made worse by a too-green surgeon. And now I've come home, and I'm meant to let everyone fete me as the conquering hero? I can't conceive of anything more distasteful."

She nodded slowly. "That's certainly one point of view."

"There can be no other."

"There can," she said.

Jack gave her a dark look.

Bea didn't allow it to intimidate her. "Even if all you say is true, it doesn't negate your being a hero," she said. "You must have plenty of heroic moments in your past."

"In the past, precisely," Jack replied. "No one cares a whit about those heroics. People only care about what a chap has done lately. It doesn't matter how extraordinarily he did something before if his most recent endeavor has blown up in his face."

She privately acknowledged the truth of his words. But it wouldn't do to encourage him. Not when he was in his current frame of mind. "You speak of people in general terms. Yet, we're talking of your family."

A gentle wind drifted over the banks of the stream, rustling the leaves in the trees and making the forget-me-nots dance in the grass.

"With family, it's worse," Jack said.

"How so?" Bea asked, wrapping her cashmere shawl more firmly about her.

"Your family perpetually judges you for your latest accomplishments, while at the same time forcing you to serve a lifelong sentence for the idiocies of your youth." Jack stabbed the tip of his cane into the grass. "I could be promoted countless times, receive a passel of medals for bravery, and James would still see me as the same witless scoundrel who used to meddle with village girls and engage in ill-conceived wagers."

*Meddle with village girls?*

Bea drew back. "Er, what do you mean—"

"I was a lad. I did what lads do. And far less, I might add, than most of the chaps that have been under my command in the army. But there's no shedding one's reputation with one's own family. And after what happened at Mohammerah... And what's happened with you... That reputation will be even worse."

"Forget me for a moment," Bea said.

Jack glared at her. "As if I could."

Bea's heart skipped a beat. She ignored the sensation. "It's your wrong-headed ideas about how you were injured that trouble me."

"Wrong-headed, you call them?"

"Indeed. What does it matter how you were injured if that injury took place while you were—"

"Because," he interrupted crossly, "I'd rather it had been our enemy who put an end to my glorious military career, not one of my own men. And not my bloody horse. Forget the fact that I swooned like a woman—"

Bea bristled. "Women aren't the only ones who swoon. It's a human reaction."

"Yes, very human. I'm sure there will be ballads written about it in my honor."

It was her turn to glare. "You should be grateful to be alive."

"Alive and returning to Somerset? To farm, I daresay. How excessively exciting."

"Some might say you've had enough excitement."

"Some don't know what they're talking about."

"You crave more of it?" Bea flourished her hand. "More danger? More death on the battlefields of far-off lands?"

"I enjoy feeling alive," Jack said. "Don't you?"

"I *am* alive," she replied. "Enjoyment isn't guaranteed."

"So you've said. You do what you must to survive. This included."

*This.*

Her throat tightened. She supposed it *had* been about survival. At least, initially. That's why she'd agreed to his proposition, to save herself from the ignominy of being sacked mid-voyage and left destitute—or worse. But there had been more to it even then. Bea wasn't too proud to admit it, if only to herself.

Jack Beresford was, and would always be, a hero in her eyes.

He was the only person in memory who had ever come to Bea's rescue. The only one who'd willingly stood between her and the harsh forces of the world that had been chipping away at her defenses, day by day and year by year, since she'd first struck out on her own at the age of seventeen.

No one else had ever defended her. Had ever seen to her comforts, or cared a single jot if she was too cold.

That there had been a time limit on it all didn't negate what it meant to her.

"I daresay you think it unwise of me to have agreed to such a ruse," she said. "The risk is great. More so for me than it is for you."

"But you took it anyway," Jack said. "Why?"

Bea didn't have to search her mind for the answer. It was staring her straight in the face. "Perhaps," she said, "you and I aren't so very different after all."

JACK UTTERED A DRY CHUCKLE. HER ASSERTION was comical on its surface. And yet... She wasn't entirely wrong. "No," he acknowledged. "We're not, are we?"

"Rather strange," she said.

He regarded her in the morning sunlight that filtered through the trees. "Rather nice, actually."

A delicate blush seeped into Bea's cheeks. She was wearing the shawl he'd given her. It softened her appearance. And there was something about her hair too. It wasn't in its usual severe coil of tightly secured plaits. It was in a loose knot at her nape, with stray tendrils left to frame her face. Sitting beside him, here at Beasley, in the clear light that glittered off the trickling stream—

She looked beautiful.

She *was* beautiful.

After his interview with James last night, Jack had lain awake in his room for hours, thinking about her. He'd imagined her at his side during the hectic week to come, meeting his family, and accompanying him to the ball. He was used to having her with him, as his ally and friend. She made him feel strong. Capable. As though he had something worthwhile to stand for. To fight for.

But she hadn't agreed to any of this.

The swell of her full skirts was brushing up against his leg. He took a fold of the worn gray wool between his fingers. It wasn't the same as taking her hand. Certainly not the same as kissing her. But it was better than nothing.

"Forgive my complaining," he said. "I rarely get maudlin."

"Not at all," Bea said. "You've certainly heard me complaining about my situation enough."

"Mine isn't nearly so dire—except to my pride."

"Yes, well... families can be difficult," she said. "Or so I've observed during my years as a governess. I expect it's different if the family is your own."

Jack frowned. He didn't like to think of her being an outsider. Always on the periphery. Never included. Never secure. "You have no memories of life with your own family?"

"Only happy ones," Bea said. "Although, I confess, they are a little faded now."

"My family is a happy one, too. Just complicated." He gave her skirts a tug. "Not to worry. It's nothing I can't manage."

The color in Bea's cheeks turned a shade darker. She pulled her skirts from his grasp. "Must you disarrange my person in such a cavalier manner?"

Jack smiled at the tartness in her words. If not for her blushes, he'd think she was irritated with him. "I enjoy disarranging your person."

"Really, Jack. How are we to converse if you—"

"Yes, yes. Point taken. You were saying?"

"*You* were saying." She straightened her skirts. "I believe you were about to tell me what it is that we're going to do about this mess."

Jack's mood sobered. "*We're* not going to do anything," he said. "This is my problem, not yours."

Her gaze jolted to his. "But I thought—"

"You're right," he said. "It's best that you slip away this morning. I'll take you to a hotel in Maidenbridge myself. It won't be as far removed from Beasley as if you'd stayed in Southampton, but in many ways it's better."

Bea shook her head. "Jack—"

"You'll be safer nearby, for one. And for another, I can more easily reach you with your reference and the direction of your new employer. I'll speak with Hannah today."

Her eyes narrowed. "After you've told her that I've surreptitiously abandoned you?"

"No one in my family will blame you for that," he said. "They'll think you an uncommonly sensible female. As for the rest of it... They can cancel the ball. Send word to the villagers that we've broken up. It will be a nine days' scandal, but I've endured worse, and you'll be well out of it."

Bea didn't appear at all mollified by this fact. Quite the reverse.

She stood abruptly. "And *this* is what you'd have me do? Slink away with my tail between my legs, leaving you to face the whole of your family on your own?"

Jack's brows notched in a defensive scowl. "It was *you* who suggested it."

She folded her arms across her midsection, pacing the muddy bank in front of him. "Yes, a very practical plan," she muttered. "As well as being faithless, cowardly, and—"

"You're talking nonsense," he said. "We both know that the wisest course—"

She came to a sudden halt. "What if I didn't go?"

Jack's breath stopped in his chest. *"What?"*

"What if I stayed until after the ball?" she asked.

He regarded her warily, even as his pulse quickened. "Why on earth would you?"

"To help you," she said.

"Yes, but why subject yourself—"

"To *help* you," she said again. "You helped me on the Pera."

"We helped each other."

"So you say. But I've never thought our positions equal. The service you did me has always been far greater than the one I did for you."

"No, it hasn't," Jack said. "Not in terms of—"

"In terms of money. You paid for my passage and my stateroom. Not to mention my rail fare in a first-class compartment, and all my meals—"

"Bea, will you stop talking rot?"

"It isn't rot." She stood over him, the shawl he'd given her drooping from her shoulders. A stray lock of hair curled around her cheek. "It's a debt. And one I mean to repay."

Jack stared at her. "Good God. You're serious."

"I like it no better than you," she said. "I obviously don't fit here, and I—"

"If I say you fit, you fit," Jack interrupted with sudden fierceness. "And who the devil would know better than I?"

"Your oldest brother," she replied promptly. "Your parents. The rest of your siblings."

Jack gripped his cane, using it to get to his feet. His knee twinged sharply, sending a spike of pain up his leg. He gritted his teeth against it. "Don't judge them by St. Clare's ridiculous standards. Wait until you meet Ivo and Kate. You'll see that I'm speaking the truth."

Bea took a step back as he came to stand in front of her. Her blush returned, but she didn't shy away from his gaze.

She met his eyes boldly. "It little matters to our plan. Our fake engagement will only continue for a few days longer."

Jack marked the subtle alteration in her color and the slight unevenness in her breath. His body responded to every change, his blood warming and his heart losing its rhythm.

"And you're not to think any of this is an effort to trap you," Bea added. "No matter what foolish thought I may have given voice to on the docks."

"What foolish thought?" he asked her.

"The one I mentioned in the moments just before you caught sight of your brother," she said. "But perhaps you didn't hear me? You were that alarmed once you saw him."

Jack smiled slowly. He *had* been alarmed to see James. But he hadn't lost all his faculties. "I heard you."

Her cheeks blazed. "Did you?"

"I did," he said. "And I didn't think it foolish."

She briefly dropped her gaze, flustered. "It was a hypothetical, merely. Governesses pose them all the time when making arguments. I didn't mean—"

"Bea—"

"I was simply making a point," she said. "I shouldn't like it to cause any misapprehensions about our agreement."

Jack felt a disconcerting rush of tenderness for her. "I have no misapprehensions about you. On that you may rest assured."

"Good." Her eyes tentatively lifted back to his. "Not that it would matter one jot, when the end result will be the same."

"An amicable breakup?"

"Exactly," she said.

Jack reached to adjust her shawl, pulling the drooping

cashmere back over her shoulder. He was no longer sure about end results. About her, or about himself. All he knew was that, whatever this was, he wanted it to last a while longer.

"If you're certain that's what you desire," he said.

Bea's throat bobbed on a delicate swallow. She managed a small nod. "It is."

# Chapter Twenty-Two

"Would you like to come to our tea party, Miss Layton?"

Bea stopped at the top of the stairs, her footsteps arrested by the tiny voice behind her. Turning, she came face to face with Lord and Lady St. Clare's youngest daughter, Charlotte.

The little girl stood outside the closed door of one of the rooms along the hall, dressed in a frilly white frock, with an overlarge matron's cap haphazardly perched atop her auburn curls.

Bea suppressed a smile. When she and Jack had returned from their rendezvous by the stream, they'd breakfasted with the family before repairing to the drawing room where Jack had dispersed his trunkful of gifts. Among them had been a miniature tea set for the girls.

"I would be delighted," she said. "You must let me know when—"

"Now," Charlotte said.

"Oh!" Bea cast a glance down the staircase. No one was

waiting for her there. Not Jack, anyway. After giving his gifts, he'd gone off with his brother for another of their talks.

Bea had spent what remained of the morning in company with Hannah—and what seemed to be an ever-expanding pack of dogs—being given a tour of the house and grounds.

"My husband and Jack have much to catch up on," Hannah had explained. "Estate matters and so forth. It needn't trouble you."

Bea hadn't been so sure of that. Indeed, she suspected, just as she had last night, that *she* was the chief topic of conversation between the brothers.

Hannah, for her part, had done her best to dispel Bea's worries, keeping her busy in the house's picture gallery, music room, and library, and tramping through the uncommonly beautiful (if somewhat muddy) rose gardens.

Bea had only come upstairs to change her gown before the other Beresfords arrived. According to Hannah, they were due any moment.

"I'm not sure your mother can spare me," Bea said to Charlotte.

"Mama can certainly spare you," Charlotte replied with all the airy certainty of a seasoned society hostess. "I would invite her, but we already have too many guests."

Another smile curved Bea's lips. "Do you, indeed?"

"Agatha is pouring. And there's Frances, Wilhelmina, and Gertrude." Charlotte set her hand on the doorknob. "If you want anything to eat, you must come now. Wilhelmina has already had two of the sandwiches."

Bea came to a decision. It wasn't a difficult one, given the inducement. "Very well," she said. "After you."

Charlotte beamed. She opened the door a crack and, angling her body sideways, slipped into the room.

Bea followed via the same method into what appeared to be the children's nursery. It was the size of two large rooms put together, decorated in shades of pale pink, with rose-bud-patterned paper hangings and diaphanous ruffled curtains. The furnishings were all child sized, including the linen-draped table by the window. Charlotte's new tea service was arrayed there, along with an iced ring cake, a plate of sandwiches, and a tiered tray of petit fours.

Agatha stood beside the table, filling the cups from the dainty painted porcelain teapot.

But it wasn't that which startled a laugh out of Bea.

It was the sight of the three small dogs milling near the table—a fawn pug, a black terrier, and a curly-tailed ball of brown fluff—each of whom wore a cap similar to the ones worn by Charlotte and her sister.

Agatha shot a severe look in Bea's direction. "Don't laugh at them. You'll hurt their feelings."

"They don't like their caps," Charlotte explained. She hurried forward to adjust the one on the pug's broad brow. "Except for Frances. She loves to dress up. Don't you, Frances?"

The pug cheerfully licked Charlotte's cheek.

"Forgive me," Bea said. "I didn't mean to offend them."

"Mama says we mustn't remark on people's appearances," Agatha said. "Except to compliment them."

"Wise advice." Bea joined them at the table. The curly-tailed dog jumped up on her skirts, giving a bark of greeting. Bea reached to pet its head. "Will you not introduce us?" she asked the girls.

"That's Gertrude," Charlotte said. "And this is

Wilhelmina. She doesn't like to be petted. She only attends for the cakes. See?" She offered one of the petit fours to the terrier. The small dog snapped it up, narrowly missing the little girl's fingers.

"Goodness!" Bea exclaimed. "Do be careful!"

"Papa says Wilhelmina's manners are atrocious," Charlotte said. "But Mama and Grandmama say we must be patient with her."

"Do you have any other dogs I should be aware of?" Bea asked. "I thought I'd seen all of them."

There had been the three large dogs last night. And then, during her tour of the house and grounds, Bea had met two more.

"We have eight house dogs," Agatha informed her. "But there are more on the estate."

"Our steward has two sheepdogs," Charlotte volunteered. "And the stablemaster has a great big mastiff."

Agatha directed Bea to a diminutive chair. "You may sit down."

Bea obliged her, though she didn't entirely trust that the chair would hold her weight. Gertrude continued to dance around her hem, while Frances panted and Wilhelmina eyed the ring cake.

"I shall pour," Agatha said imperiously. She addressed Charlotte: "You may serve the sandwiches."

"WHERE IS THIS MYSTERIOUS FIANCÉE OF YOURS?" Kate demanded the moment she stepped down from her carriage. "I'm dying to meet her." She embraced Jack with characteristic exuberance, only mildly inhibited by the growing protrusion of her belly. She and her husband, Charles, were expecting their fourth child in the summer.

Jack hugged her in return. It had been three years since he'd seen his little sister. Neither time nor motherhood had altered her. With her glossy mink tresses and stubbornly cleft little chin, she was still the same firebrand who had, in childhood, been his frequent collaborator in various foolhardy endeavors.

"Miss Layton is here somewhere," he said.

Jack had left her midmorning to go off with James. An unavoidable inconvenience. It was James who had been managing Marston Priory in Jack's absence. The two of them had much to discuss. They'd be talking still if James hadn't seen the Heywoods' carriage approaching through his study window.

"She went upstairs to change," Hannah said. "She'll be down directly." Standing on the gravel drive, along with her husband, she was attempting to corral the children—both the Heywood's and her own.

Nicholas and Arthur had run out to meet their cousins the moment they'd arrived, hailing the Heywood brood with whoops and shrieks. The three Heywood children— Edward, Felicity, and Delphia—were slightly better behaved. But only slightly. They were all chattering at once, vying for Jack's attention and each other's.

"Are Agatha and Charlotte not at home?" Felicity asked Nicholas.

"They're in the nursery," Nicholas said.

"Having one of their silly tea parties," Arthur added. "Edward! Come and see the bow and arrow that Uncle Jack brought me."

"What about our gifts, Uncle Jack?" Delphia asked. "You did bring us something, didn't you?"

"Your gifts are forthcoming," Jack told the little Heywoods. "I have them in one of my trunks."

A cheer went up.

"Come into the house, children," Hannah said, urging them forward. "Mrs. Kirby has a surprise for you in the kitchens."

Old Mrs. Kirby, who had been the housekeeper at Beasley Park since Jack was a lad, awaited the children at the top of the steps. "This way, my dears," she encouraged them. "Cook has made something special for you."

Amid all the chaos, Jack turned to greet Charles Heywood. The tall, raven-haired former naval captain was as solemn as his wife and children were spirited. At first glance, one wouldn't think that he and Kate had anything in common, yet the two of them had fallen deeply in love when they'd met. And they were still in love, as far as Jack was aware.

"You'd think they hadn't seen each other in years," Charles said, flashing a bemused smile at the departing children.

James chuckled. "As opposed to at least once every fortnight."

"The benefits of living so close to one another," Kate said. She linked her arm through Jack's as they all made their way to the house. "Benefits that Jack and Miss Layton can now share. When they have children—"

"Kate," Jack objected. "I'm not even married yet. Perhaps you might refrain from organizing the social calendars of my nonexistent children?"

"Nonexistent *now*," Kate conceded. "But not for long.

Not if your marriage is indeed a love match like Hannah and Meg suspect."

Jack's jaw tightened imperceptibly. He loved his sisters-in-law, but how in blazes would either of them know how he felt about Bea? Meg hadn't even met her yet. And Hannah had only made her acquaintance last night.

It was all just supposition on their parts, based on the suddenness of his engagement. In incidences of haste, or inequalities in social standing, love was generally the operating force.

Either that or scandal.

"Besides," Kate went on. "You must indulge me in my condition." She called to her husband: "Isn't that right, my love?"

"It's certainly become my motto," Charles replied dutifully.

"A wise man," James remarked. He set his hand at Hannah's waist, exchanging a warm glance with her as they ascended the stone steps after the still-chattering children.

Theirs was another love match, the embers of which were still burning brightly, even after four children and over a decade of marriage.

Once, Jack might have been jealous. Just as he'd sometimes been jealous of Kate's and Ivo's blissful unions. They had fallen in love when they were young, with marriage and children coming soon after.

Jack's own life had followed a different pattern. He hadn't met the girl he wanted to marry in his youth. Hadn't ever fallen in love. Until quite recently, he'd begun to believe he never would.

"Now," Kate said. "If only Ivo and Meg would give up their house in London and move home to the West Country. They'd be far happier here than in town, don't you think? And then all the children could be together in one big—"

Her voice was drowned out by the clatter of carriage wheels.

"Speak of the devil," Charles said.

A hired coach and four rolled briskly up the drive. Two ginger-haired, freckle-faced lads of ten and twelve were peering eagerly out the window. It was Ivo and Meg's boys, Aldrick and Oscar. They had their mothers coloring—the only remnant left of Meg's father, the late Sir Frederick Burton-Smythe, who had once been the mortal enemy of Jack's own father.

Hannah and James turned on the steps. "What impeccable timing!" Hannah said. "That will be Ivo's doing."

"Some new-fangled calculation, knowing him," James replied. He accompanied his wife back down the drive as the coach ground to a halt.

The two boys tumbled out first. They charged Jack with a duo of merry shrieks loud enough to rival that of their Heywood and Beresford cousins. "Uncle Jack! Uncle Jack!"

Ivo and Meg followed their children out of the carriage.

"Leave off, boys," Ivo said to his sons. "Don't knock your uncle down."

The lads detached themselves just enough to make room for their father who strode forward to enfold Jack in a crushing hug. "My God it's good to see you," he said.

Jack hugged his brother back. "And you."

"How's the leg? Any improvement since the last surgery?"

"Not much. I require rest apparently."

Ivo smiled broadly, the sunlight glinting off of his silver-framed spectacles. "Whatever that is."

"Welcome home, J-Jack," Meg stammered as she hugged Jack in turn. "You look well."

Jack kissed her cheek. "So do you, Meg. How are you? How are the boys?"

"Happy," she said. "Happy in London. Happy to see you."

"Happy, full stop," Ivo appended with a grin. "So? When do I get to meet your Miss Layton? She *is* here, isn't she?"

"My question exactly," Kate said.

"She's inside," Hannah told them. "And she's lovely."

"I'd expect nothing less," Kate said. "Jack was always particularly discerning in that regard."

"Enough of that," Jack chided, only partially in jest. "You'll put me to the blush."

"Discernment is nothing to be ashamed of," Kate retorted. "It means you have standards. So should we all."

"Where are Nicholas and Arthur?" Aldrick asked, trotting up the steps alongside the adults.

"They've gone down to the kitchens with Mrs. Kirby," James said.

Hannah gave the boys a conspiratorial smile. "There's a rumor that Cook has made chocolate biscuits."

The boys jumped up and down. "Can we go down, Mama?" they asked Meg.

"Of course," Meg said. "If Aunt Hannah allows it."

"Oh yes," Hannah said. "Edward, Felicity, and Delphia are already there. And Charlotte and Agatha will be joining you shortly."

Jack entered the hall with his sister and the others. A

footman closed the door behind them. Kate relinquished Jack's arm to remove her bonnet and cloak. Charles, Meg, and Ivo similarly divested themselves.

"I'll go up to fetch Bea and the girls," Hannah said. She looked to her husband. "My dear? If you would be so good as to take everyone into the drawing—"

"*Stop thief!*" Agatha screamed out from the landing.

All of the adults froze where they stood. Seven sets of eyes jerked upward in time to see Bea sprinting toward the staircase in a flurry of gray wool skirts. Agatha and Charlotte were running after her, their white muslin caps askew.

"Don't let her take it!" Charlotte cried, very near tears.

"Stop her!" Agatha shouted. "You can't allow her to steal!"

Jack's heart leapt into his throat. For a moment, he thought—

And then a little black terrier plunged down the staircase at breakneck speed. It was holding something large in its mouth. Something nearly as big as it was.

Good lord! Was that a ring cake?

"Don't fret!" Bea called back to the girls. "I almost have her!" Clutching her skirts in one hand, she raced down the steps two at a time. "Wilhelmina, you naughty girl! Come here this instant!"

The terrier evaded Bea's grasp. Eyes bulging wildly, the little dog dodged and weaved, all while holding the ring cake firmly in its jaws.

One of Bea's booted feet slipped dangerously on a marble step.

"*Bloody hell.*" Jack rushed forward without thought, nearly losing his own footing in the process. He reached for

Bea in the selfsame second the terrier flew by, knocking his cane out from under him.

Agatha and Charlotte screamed as Jack pitched forward. He caught Bea in his arms before she fell and, twisting his body, brought them down safely on the steps in a sitting position.

The terrier didn't lose stride. She flew down the last steps undaunted, preparing to run the gauntlet of humans who barred her path.

"James!" Hannah exclaimed. "Grab her!"

James deftly caught the dog as she darted past, sweeping her up in his arms. His icy countenance betrayed not a glimmer of humor. "Bad form, Wilhelmina," he said, plucking the iced cake from her teeth. "One never steals from one's hosts."

"Well done, Papa!" the little girls cheered.

Jack sat back on the step, with Bea halfway in his lap. Her hair had come loose from its pins, and perspiration dotted her brow. A rueful smile danced in her eyes.

She was opening her mouth to say something to him when she belatedly registered the presence of the new arrivals standing at the bottom of the staircase with Hannah and James. They were regarding Bea with expressions that ranged from shocked amusement to outright dismay. One could only imagine what they were thinking.

In that moment, Jack didn't care. All he knew was that Bea was in his arms, and that nothing in his life had ever felt more right.

"Bea," he said. "Allow me to introduce my little sister Kate and her husband, Charles Heywood; and that's my older brother Ivo, and his wife Meg." A ridiculous smile tugged at Jack's mouth, impossible to suppress. "Everyone, this is my Bea."

# Chapter Twenty-Three

M y Bea.

The two words played over and over again in Bea's mind in a continuous refrain all through tea in the drawing room, another round of gift giving, and a foray into the gardens so the children could test their skill with the various trifles Jack had given them. It was still echoing in her head during dinner, and afterward as Jack's family engaged in several boisterous rounds of charades.

Jack had uttered the words with a grin, and seemingly without thinking. But they had sounded sincere enough that, several hours later, Bea's heart had still failed to regain its normal rhythm.

She cast him a discreet glance as they sat together on the tufted damask-covered sofa in front of the marble fireplace in Beasley Park's silk-papered drawing room. What an excellent actor he was. The things he said. The way he looked at her. The casual manner in which he'd taken her hand and kissed it when she offered the winning guess during their final game of charades.

He gave his family every impression that he cared for her. Indeed, his actions were so persuasive, Bea could almost believe it herself. The fact both vexed and impressed her by turns.

As for the rest of the Beresfords, they were nothing like Bea had expected. Oh, they were handsome enough, to be sure, as well as being impeccably dressed. And they certainly hadn't refrained from asking Bea questions about where she was from and how she and Jack had met. But they didn't appear to look down their noses at her for all that. They weren't outwardly rude or disdainful. They weren't even as top lofty as Lord St. Clare had initially seemed. On the contrary, they were loud and opinionated, frequently talking over each other, and engaging in good-humored banter.

They also didn't relegate their offspring to the nursery for the whole of the evening. All nine of the children had joined the adults for charades. The game had soon devolved into gleeful laughter and energetic verbal sparring as a result. The Beresfords, it transpired, were a competitive lot. Lady Kate was still lamenting her loss over coffee, long after the children had been sent off to bed.

She sat on the sofa opposite Bea and Jack, clad in a stunning dark blue silk dinner dress with a loose-fitting midsection. She balanced her coffee cup on the swell of her belly. "The teams were poorly organized," she said. "That's your fault, Ivo."

Ivo straightened from petting one of the wolfhounds. It was sprawled on the carpet near the settee where he and his wife were seated, along with four other sleeping dogs. "I disagree," he said. "The teams were perfectly arranged. You thought so too before you started to lose."

Kate narrowed her eyes at her brother. "You make me out to be a sore loser."

"You *sound* like a sore loser," St. Clare remarked quietly. He stood by his wife's chair near the crackling fire, one hand resting lightly on her shoulder.

"Only because I'm not at my best," Kate retorted. "Be warned. Once this baby comes, and I am myself again, I shall show you no mercy."

"It's not Ivo you should be worried about, sweetheart," Charles said from his place beside her. "It was Miss Layton who trounced you."

"And whose idea was it to put Miss Layton on Jack's team if not Ivo's?" Kate demanded.

"Miss Layton will always be on my team," Jack said. "A fiancé's privilege."

Bea's heart thumped hard. She forced herself to take another drink of her coffee. It was rich and strong. Everything Lord and Lady St. Clare had served today had been equally luxurious. Though not in a strictly traditional sense. Dinner, for example, had contained a great many more vegetable dishes than it had mutton, chicken, or beef.

"Hannah abstains from all animal flesh," Meg Beresford had explained to Bea at the table. Married to Ivo, she was a soft-spoken, red-haired lady, with a delicate stammer. "She's a member of the Vegetarian Society. She claims it's a question of conscience."

Bea had no knowledge of vegetarianism in England, but she was quite familiar with it in India. There it was a matter of religion—and compassion. It seemed strange to find the practice observed here in the Somerset countryside, among the descendants of countesses and earls.

Or perhaps not so strange, the more Bea observed them. For all their wealth and pedigree, they struck her as people of principle. Of conscience and compassion. *And* of decided opinion.

"That's not how it works," Kate said to Jack.

"The loser's lament," Jack retorted without malice.

Kate scoffed at the accusation. "Spouses and sweethearts have an unfair advantage. It's why Charles and I can't be on the same team."

Jack leaned back on the sofa, his injured leg stretched out in front of him. "Charades are dull sport in any case. When I'm fully healed and you're safely delivered of my new niece or nephew, you and I shall have a proper contest."

Kate's face immediately brightened. "A race?"

Jack smiled. "Why not?"

"I can think of several reasons," Charles said ominously.

Kate flashed her husband an arch look before returning her attention to her brother. "Have you ridden since...?"

Jack's smile dimmed. "I wouldn't call it riding, but yes. I've been on horse." He lowered his coffee cup back to its saucer with a soft clink. "I was thinking of taking one out tomorrow."

"To anywhere in particular?" St. Clare asked.

Jack met his oldest brother's gaze. "To the Priory."

"Marston Priory is Jack's estate near Exford," Kate said to Bea. "It used to belong to my mother's side of the family, but Jack bought it outright some years ago. My brother James has had the running of it."

"Until now." Jack returned his coffee cup to the silver tray on the low table in front of the sofa. "Henceforward,

I'll be the one managing things. I'll ride out in the morning to get the lay of the land."

There was a protracted silence.

"I wouldn't advise it," St. Clare said. "Better you should take a carriage."

Jack shrugged off the suggestion. "It's but six miles each way. Seven at most. I could manage it blindfolded."

"We're not talking about your vision," St. Clare said. "We're talking about your leg."

Hannah covered St. Clare's hand gently with her own. "My father was able to ride soon after his leg injury. He still can, though he's older, and arthritis has set in."

"I suspect our mother has something to do with that," Charles said. "The two of them often ride together."

"A good point," Kate said to Jack. "You shouldn't go alone. If you must ride out, take Maberly with you. Or perhaps Charles or Ivo can—"

"I was thinking of taking Bea," Jack said.

Bea felt the eyes of everyone else turn upon her. A flush of embarrassment crept up her throat. "But...I can't ride."

One would think she'd just declared that she couldn't breathe air.

"Can't ride!" Kate exclaimed. "You're not serious?"

Bea managed a faint smile. "Is that so shocking?"

"We're a horse-going family on all sides," Ivo said. "My maternal grandfather, Squire Honeywell, was famous for his bloodstock, and my father's family kept a notable stable. Charles's family too, and Meg's. We all have that in common."

Bea carefully placed her cup and saucer on the tray beside Ivo's. She was already lacking in so many respects. She didn't have the right clothes, the right looks, the right pedigree. She'd thought for a moment that by prevailing at charades she'd begun to fit in, but not anymore, apparently. "I'm sorry," she said. "There weren't many opportunities to ride in India."

Not for a governess.

"Have you ever b-been on a horse?" Meg asked.

"A few times," Bea said. "Nothing to mention."

"Then you can't even ride a little?" Kate asked.

"I'm afraid not," Bea replied.

"I'll teach you," Jack said.

Bea's gaze jerked to his. Her pulse gave an erratic leap. "Oh no," she objected. "You wouldn't wish to waste your time doing that."

"Nothing I'd rather do," he said gallantly.

She shook her head. "Really, Jack. I'd only slow you down."

"I'll be slow enough on my own until I get my bearings. It will be the perfect conditions for you to learn." Jack looked to St. Clare and Hannah. "Do you still have that old mare the children learned to ride on?"

"Nightshade?" Hannah asked. "Why, yes."

"She's nearly twenty, Jack," Kate protested. "She hasn't got any pep."

"Pep isn't required," Jack said. "So long as she's steady and reliable."

A dozen objections sprang to Bea's lips, but she had no opportunity to make them. The Beresfords were off on another subject with lightning speed, discussing past horses and past races they'd had with each other. Before long, it was time to retire. Even then, Bea had no opportunity of waylaying Jack, for Meg quietly commandeered her attention as they exited the drawing room.

"I presume you d-don't have a riding habit," she said.

"Indeed, I do not," Bea replied.

"I'd be happy to lend you mine. It will be a little too big on you, but that's easily remedied. My lady's maid is capable of performing miracles."

Some of the tension in Bea's muscles eased. That was one worry dealt with at least. "Thank you. You're very kind."

Meg smiled. "Not at all."

---

BEA SENT UP A SILENT PRAYER FOR HER OWN safety as Maberly tossed her up into the sidesaddle. Jack came forward immediately after, supplanting his batman at the black mare's side. He helped Bea put her foot into the stirrup as she struggled to get her other leg over the pommel.

One of the grooms was at the mare's head, holding her bridle. The mare herself stood quiet, except for the occasional impatient strike of one steel-shod hoof against the cobblestones of the stable yard.

Bea could feel every twitch of the creature's back as she settled herself into the saddle. "She's excessively tall, isn't she?" she remarked breathlessly.

"She's fifteen hands," Jack said. "Rather smallish." He was dressed for riding in Bedford cord breeches and a blue broadcloth coat. "Here, take the reins. No, don't pull on them. And don't use them to hold on. That's not what they're for."

Bea followed his instructions, all the while aware that she had absolutely no control over the animal. It was only the illusion of control. And in a borrowed riding costume besides. The dark green habit that Meg had lent her was fashionably elegant, with a smart little jacket that nipped at Bea's waist and a heavy drape of skirts that flowed over her legs in a graceful sweep of fabric.

"Seven miles each way, did you say?" she asked as Jack went to his own horse. It was a blood bay gelding, much larger than Bea's mount, with a wild light in its eye.

"About that much," Jack replied.

Maberly assisted Jack into his saddle, with the aid of a wooden mounting block. Jack's jaw was tight, his face flinching as he bent his injured leg to set his boot in the stirrup.

Bea found herself wincing in unison. "It can't be good to bend your knee so much."

"I'm supposed to bend it. It's the only way it will heal properly." Gathering the reins, Jack turned his horse toward hers. "Shall we set off?"

"Are you entirely sure it's a good idea?" Bea asked. "What if something should happen along the way? What if you need to dismount or—"

"There are grooms at the Priory stables." Jack paused, frowning. "And Maberly is coming with us."

Bea's brows lifted. This was the first she'd heard of it.

Across the yard, Maberly disappeared into the stone stable block. He emerged seconds later on the back of a dun-colored horse.

"He'll follow behind," Jack said. "If something happens—which it won't—he'll be on hand to assist us."

It was a relief, though Bea was reluctant to show it. She had the impression that Jack wasn't pleased to have his batman's assistance. Doubtless it was a blow to his pride. He was an independent sort of gentlemen, as evidenced by his long career in the army, and his equally long period of bachelorhood. He didn't want anyone looking after him or interfering with his life.

He circled his horse around Bea's mare. "Loosen your reins a notch," he told her. "And follow me."

At first, Bea did just that, keeping a horse's length between them as she'd once heard a riding master tell one of her young charges to do. But that was the wrong thing, apparently.

"You needn't hang back," Jack called to her. "Nudge her with your heel. Bring her up on my right side."

"So close?"

"We can ride two abreast for most of the way. The horses won't object. Copper and Nightshade are old friends."

"Very well." Bea pressed her heel against Nightshade's side. The mare picked up her pace, advancing quickly to walk alongside her stablemate.

Jack's mouth tipped at one corner. "Not so difficult, is it?"

Bea huffed. "Speak for yourself."

"I won't say it's particularly easy at present, but I'll get there again, never fear."

"You love riding as much as the rest of your family?"

"The Cavalry would have been a dreadful trial if I didn't."

Together they rode down the drive, and through the gates that led to a tree-lined country lane. Maberly followed a distance behind them, close enough to be on hand if anything dire should occur, but far enough away to assure their privacy.

Soon Beasley Park faded into the distance. Trees closed around them, their branches curving over the lane in a graceful arch. The horses' hooves clip-clopped steadily on the hard-packed earth.

"So," Jack said at length, "what do you make of my family?"

Bea didn't hesitate. "I like them."

"Do you?"

"I do." She readjusted her reins between her gloved fingers. "Did you think I wouldn't?"

"I knew you would," he said. And then: "I hoped."

A resurgence of butterflies tickled Bea's stomach at the husky note in Jack's voice. "They're easy to like," she said. "So very kind and genuine. I'm amazed that—" She stopped herself.

Jack flashed her a glance. "What?"

"That they don't mind my being a governess," she said.

He smiled, as though something had amused him.

Bea resumed looking straight ahead. The road was on a gentle incline, heading toward a small rise in the distance. "But I suppose they do mind. They're just too polite to show it."

"They *can* be polite," he said. "But if they disliked you, you'd know it." He slowed his horse when Bea began to fall behind, waiting for her to catch up. "As far as your being a governess... We Beresfords aren't as high in the instep in that regard as people might think."

Bea brought Nightshade back alongside Jack's horse. The little mare boldly stretched out her face to nuzzle the gelding. He bumped her nose in return.

"The family of an earl is expected to have certain standards," Bea said.

Jack scratched his horse's withers. A thoughtful line etched his brow. "My father wasn't always the earl. He wasn't always the heir to an earldom either. For a time, when he was a lad, he had no knowledge of his true lineage. For quite a few years, actually. He spent them working as a stableboy at Beasley Park. It's where he met my mother."

Bea couldn't conceal her surprise. "You're not serious?"

"As the grave." Jack guided his horse up the rise. "It's our family secret. Though not much of one, if you ask me. Not when there are some blackguards out there who still whisper that my father's claim to the earldom is illegitimate. Which," he added darkly, "would mean that St. Clare's claim is illegitimate too. It's why he's so sensitive about anything that might tarnish the family name."

Bea kept pace with Jack on her mare as they crested the hill. She didn't know what to say. It was all too astonishing.

Jack gave her a wry smile. "So, if St. Clare looks at you askance, you can chalk it up to that. He's always on his guard for adventurers and the like. It's nothing personal."

"Does he think I'm an adventurer?" Bea asked.

"I wouldn't take it personally."

Bea's heart sank. "I see."

"You don't," Jack said.

"But if he—"

"It has nothing to do with you. It's about him. And about his propensity to listen to meddling busybodies whose only purpose in life is to stir up trouble."

Her brows notched. "What do you mean—"

"It doesn't matter in any event," Jack interrupted. "St. Clare is already warming to you."

She gave a snort of disbelief.

"He is," Jack said. "After your valiant effort to save his

daughters' tea cake? The way you complimented Hannah's vegetarian dishes at dinner, and the way you jumped right in with us at charades? If ever he did think you an adventuress, he knows better now."

"Yet, I am lying to him," Bea said. "To all of them."

"No more than I am."

"That doesn't make it any less despicable." Bea guided Nightshade closer to Copper. "Perhaps you shouldn't have told me."

"About my father?"

"You said it's a family secret."

"So I did." Jack squinted up into the sun. "By the by, my sister took me aside this morning and posed me a question. I said I'd put it to you."

Bea tensed. Of all the Beresford relations she'd met, she was most wary of Lady Kate. Jack's younger sister was hot-blooded and unpredictable, with a propensity for speaking her mind. One never knew what she was going to say.

"What question?" Bea asked.

"She, Meg, and Hannah want to take you to a dressmaker's shop in Maidenbridge to help you choose a few things. A gown for the ball and so forth."

Bea's mouth went dry. "I suppose it's obvious that I'm in dire need."

Jack's gaze swept over her. "When was the last time you bought a new dress for yourself?"

"What does that matter?" she asked. "I can't afford a new one regardless."

"You wouldn't be paying," he said. "I would."

Bea opened her mouth to object.

Jack forestalled her. "As your fiancé—"

"But you're not my—" Bea broke off, remembering

Maberly's presence behind them. She dropped her voice. "You can't buy me *clothes*. It's entirely inappropriate."

"It's costuming for your role," Jack said. "Remember?"

She had to exert herself not to clench hard on the reins. "What can I say to that?"

"I don't know. Thank you?"

She glared at him in silence.

His mouth quirked. "My sister and sisters-in-law are determined. I find it best to acquiesce to their wishes. I advise you to do the same. The expense won't bankrupt me. My brother informs me that my estate is earning handsomely." His smile broadened. "You may be pleased to hear that your fiancé is on his way to being a very rich man."

"How fortunate for my fiancé," Bea said stiffly. Sensing her precarious mood, Nightshade commenced an anxious jig beneath her. Bea's hands immediately tightened fearfully on the reins. "What is she doing?"

"You're making her anxious," Jack said. "Loosen your reins and relax your seat."

"Relax my seat? How in the world—?"

"Don't sit so rigidly. You can be straight in the saddle without pokering up."

Bea grudgingly followed his advice. Once again, it proved effective. Nightshade ceased her jig and resumed walking at Copper's side.

"Horses feel what we feel," Jack said. "If you're tense, they become tense. And if you're relaxed, they'll relax. Why do you think Copper is so happy right now, prancing along through the woods, without a care in the world?"

Bea's brows knit doubtfully. "Because you're happy?"

"Exactly," Jack said.

She exhaled. "Because you're riding again."

He didn't reply, only smiled at her.

Her pulse fluttered. Everything within her told her that he was happy being with her. But she dared not believe it. She was already in far too deep. Meeting his family. Learning his secrets. Charging new dresses to his account. Where on earth would it end?

But it would end, she knew.

Bea refused to lose sight of the fact.

"Isn't it dangerous for me to go into the village?" she asked.

"Dangerous how?"

"The more people who meet me, the greater the chance of gossip. And the greater the gossip, the more risk to my reputation as a governess."

Jack's smile faded. "You're not intending to be a governess here in Maidenbridge, are you?"

"Of course not. But—"

"Then it won't matter. Not when you're employed in Yorkshire or Northumberland or...or Inverness."

"Inverness!" A horrified laugh bubbled in her throat. "You're not intending to seek a position for me in the Scottish Highlands?"

He chuckled. "It's the farthest from Somerset I could think of."

"Is that the goal, then?" she asked. "To get me as far away from you as you can?"

Jack's eyes held hers. There was a look in them that was hard to read. "On the contrary," he said. "I mean to keep you close."

Bea's heart thumped hard. *For now*, he should have said. It was what he meant, surely. What he was implying.

Yet it wasn't what he'd said to her.

She moistened her lips as they rode on through the trees and along the edge of an open field. She debated asking Jack about their fake engagement and how it must necessarily end. But the words wouldn't come. The day was too beautiful. And she was too happy—yes, happy—here in her borrowed habit atop her borrowed horse, riding with Jack beneath the shimmering sun. It felt like where she belonged.

It was a dangerous feeling to indulge. Normally, she wouldn't allow herself to. But what was one morning of make-believe in the grand scheme of things?

"When you're more confident," Jack said. "We can canter through this stretch. We might even race if you're up for the challenge."

"And let you beat me?" Bea laughed. "No thank you."

"How do you know I would?"

"Because you obviously arm yourself to win. You have a bigger horse. A *younger* horse. You're also a better rider than I am. It would be no contest at all."

"Funny," Jack remarked. "I'd have said we're rather well matched."

Bea flashed him a speaking look.

Jack grinned, changing the subject before Bea could make a tart reply. He told her about the history of Marston Priory. He spoke about how it had been built in the late fifteenth century, and about the Hamstone used to construct it. He described the ancient gateway to the property, the vast simplicity of the great hall, and the recently refurbished tenant cottages and farms.

A beguiling picture of the place began to form in Bea's mind. But when, many miles later, the Priory at last came into view, Bea realized that her imagination had failed to do it justice.

It stood upon a rise, surrounded by a low wall, all honey-colored stone and stately elegance. A huge house, but not a cold one. The roof was partially thatched, the gardens flourishing, and the rolling lawns emerald green amid the trees.

Bea stopped her horse to stare at it, her breast swelling with longing. What would it be like to be mistress of such a house? To live here with Jack? To be the recipient of his affection? His love?

Jack was silent on his horse beside her. When at last she turned to him, she found that he was staring, not at the house, but at her. "Would you like to go inside?"

Bea smiled. "Can we?"

He smiled slowly in return. "We can do whatever we like," he said. "All this belongs to me."

# Chapter Twenty-Four

"I think she's rather perfect for you," Kate said, walking alongside Jack in the Beasley Park rose gardens.

Jack strolled at her side, with the aid of his cane. It had been two days since he'd taken Bea to the Priory. She'd loved the place, just as he'd hoped she would. And he'd been giddy as a schoolboy showing it to her, seeing it with new eyes because she was with him.

No longer had the estate seemed something to settle for. A provincial prison where he would unwillingly retire after leaving the army. It had instead seemed to be filled with possibility. A place that could be a home. That could one day lodge a family. A place where—with the right person at his side—Jack might be happy.

They'd walked through most of the house, until his aching knee had forced them to stop for tea. After that, they'd ridden over the grounds. He'd even managed to coax Bea into a trot. The picture of her face, illuminated by a radiant smile, had been plaguing him ever since.

"She has a tart tongue when she dares use it," Kate went on. "She's bold. Some might say fearless. She's good with the children, but not too rigid. She rides."

"She rides," Jack agreed. "She's gaining more confidence every day."

"And she's not a spendthrift. We had the devil of a time convincing her to charge anything to your account at the dressmaker's yesterday. In the end she could only be persuaded to a new riding habit, a dinner dress, and a gown for the ball. I tried to explain to her that she would need much more than that. There are day dresses to think of, as well as her wedding clothes. She had better purchase those in London. Unless..." Kate hesitated. "And I may be speaking out of turn, so do feel free to stop me."

"What?"

"It's only that... I have the distinct impression that this is all something of a ruse."

Jack stopped where he stood. He failed to conceal a wince. He already knew that James suspected something was amiss. But no one else had had the temerity to express their qualms to Jack directly.

It figured that it would be Kate. She knew him too well.

Jack nevertheless affected a not-very-convincing tone of indignation. "A *ruse*? Are you serious?"

Kate sighed. "So, it's true, then," she said. "The engagement isn't real."

Jack made one final effort to deter her. "You're talking nonsense."

"Not only me. James is suspicious. So is Ivo. Both of them asked me outright—"

"If my engagement is a fake one?"

"Which it is," Kate said. "Don't worry. I have no intention of telling either of them. They never did understand our little schemes." Her brow puckered. "Not that I understand this one any better."

"Kate—"

Taking his arm, she directed him to the bench beneath the arbor. "You may as well confess, Jack. The whole affair reeks of one of your larks. There's only one thing wrong."

Jack scowled at her as he sank down on the bench. "Which is?"

She sat down beside him, resting a hand on her belly. "The two of you are too dashed compatible. Which either means that Miss Layton has agreed to this escapade—which is already enough to persuade me that she's your earthly ideal—or that somewhere along the way the two of you have unwittingly fallen in—"

"*Enough*," Jack snapped. "Enough, Kate. I won't hear a word about her."

"Don't bite my head off," Kate shot back. "I like the girl!"

"So do I," Jack said. "But things are delicate."

Kate's brows elevated nearly to her hairline. "You're not saying that you have...? But that she hasn't...?" She looked at him with an expression of complete incredulity. "I don't believe it."

Jack supposed he should be flattered that his sister had so much faith in him. But it was poor consolation given his present predicament. "Believe what you will," he said. "So long as you say nothing to Bea—or to James or Ivo."

"You're forgetting someone else," Kate said. "*Two* someones."

Jack grimaced. He didn't need his sister to remind him.

Kate reminded him anyway. "Mama and Papa are

arriving tomorrow. They should be here just in time for the opening of the ball. And if you think James and Ivo and I are alert to your larks, you should know that Mama and Papa have not lost a step, even though they are old, the dears."

Jack's mother and father were in their late sixties. It *was* old, Jack conceded, but their enduring love for each other, along with a lifetime of physical activity, had kept them strong in body and young at heart.

"I'm not afraid of our parents," Jack said. "They accepted Meg into the family, didn't they? If they'll welcome her, they'll welcome anyone I choose."

"But Jack..." Kate searched his face. "*Did* you choose Miss Layton?"

Jack thought of that night on the deck of the Pera when he'd first revealed his presence to Bea as she'd been staring up at the stars. No one had made him do it. He had acted of his own accord. He'd been drawn to her even then.

He gave his sister a solemn smile. "As a matter of fact, I did."

BEA STOOD IN FRONT THE CHEVAL MIRROR IN HER bedchamber as her borrowed French lady's maid put the finishing touches on her evening ensemble. The elegant creature who stared back at Bea in the glass might as well have been a stranger. She scarcely recognized herself in her fashionable gown of amber-colored silk glacé, with its daringly low-cut neckline and its three skirts trimmed in matching amber lace.

It had been one of Hannah's. One she'd ordered that had yet to be completed. The village dressmaker had modified it for Bea, shortening the hem and taking in the bodice. It was the only way a ball gown could be finished in so short a time.

That it hadn't originally been made for Bea scarcely mattered in the end. It was the finest garment she'd ever worn, and by far the most flattering.

There was a knock on the door.

"Yes?" Bea called.

The door opened a crack. Meg peeked inside. "M-May I come in?"

"Please," Bea said.

Meg entered, closing the door behind her. She was already in her ball gown—an airy confection of pink gauze and lace. An opal-and-diamond brooch glittered at the neck of her bodice. "I came to see if there was anything you require?"

"Oh no," Bea said. "And you've already done so much, lending me your maid."

Meg smiled. "Is she n-nearly ready, Louise?"

Louise gave one final adjustment to the slim, amber silk covered belt at Bea's waist. "All finished, madame."

"Excellent, Louise. You m-may go."

"Thank you," Bea said to the maid as she withdrew. "Your mistress spoke truly. You have performed wonders."

Louise curtsied to both ladies before departing.

Meg stepped back to admire Bea. "The color suits you," she said. "So does the dress. You look beautiful in it."

Bea wouldn't go that far. Pretty, she'd have called herself. And to someone who had felt plain all of her life, to be pretty was no small thing. "You're very kind," she said. "Am I the last one down? I'm sorry if I've taken too long."

She'd had a late start getting ready. Around the Beresfords, time was a commodity in very short supply. There was always something afoot—another game, another outing, another unplanned romp with the children. Over the past several days, Bea had had little time to herself. Indeed, most nights she'd scarcely been able to make her wish on the evening star, let alone write in her journal, before falling into her bed exhausted.

Pearl would be amused. She'd often remarked that Bea spent more time documenting her life than actually living it. But not now. Not during Bea's brief idyll with Jack in Somerset. However short, this had been time for living.

"Not at all," Meg said. "Your timing is perfect. Lord and Lady Allendale have just arrived."

Bea started. "Oh!" She turned from the mirror, skirts swishing about her legs. "Should I go down now? Or—"

"No need," Meg said. "You can m-meet them at the ball."

Bea pressed a hand to her midriff. For a moment, her courage failed her. She could scarcely justify lying to Jack's siblings as it was. But to lie to his parents? An actual earl and his countess?

"They'd expected to arrive earlier in the day," Meg explained. "But their t-train was delayed. They went straight to their room to change. Kate and Ivo have already gone in to speak with them. And St. Clare, I presume. I don't know about Jack. I haven't seen him since our game of croquet on the lawn."

Neither had Bea. There had been no chance to speak

with him privately. No opportunity to strategize. They'd yet to go over the plan for their amicable breakup.

Meg collected Bea's painted fan from the dressing table. She handed it to her. "You're anxious, I can tell. You needn't be."

Bea slipped the cord of the fan over her wrist. "I'm not accustomed to meeting earls and countesses," she confessed. "I daresay I'm a little frightened of disgracing myself."

"I was afraid of Lord and Lady Allendale once too," Meg admitted. "My father didn't get on with them." She gave a short laugh. "An understatement. Our two families loathed each other. When Ivo and I m-met, neither of them was very happy about it. But Lord and Lady Allendale accepted me in the end. They're doting grandparents, and they've been a great solace to me since m-my father died."

Bea's heart twinged with compassionate understanding. She knew what it was to lose the ones you loved. "I'm sorry to hear of your father's passing."

Meg smiled. "I thank you. But it was a long while ago. Ten years, in fact. And it was n-not unexpected. My father had been ill for some time. My point is... Lord and Lady Allendale welcomed m-me into their family."

Bea's mouth tipped briefly. "Yes, but you weren't a governess before you married your husband, were you?"

Meg's eyes twinkled with humor. "I'm sure they'd rather I had been than a Burton-Smythe." She straightened a piece of lace trimming on Bea's overskirt. "Come n-now. Shall we go down together?"

Bea nodded. "Yes. But first... do you mind if we stop at the nursery? I promised to show the girls my gown."

"By all means," Meg said.

Together they went down the corridor to the nursery

where the nanny, Mrs. Lovell, was busily overseeing all nine of the children. Agatha, Charlotte, Felicity, and Delphia were in their nightgowns, knelt in front of a painted wooden dollhouse, playing with their dolls and toy animals. Nicholas was seated in the corner, in his dressing gown, reading a book. A similarly clad Arthur, Edward, Aldrick, and Oscar were at the tea table, working on one of the picture puzzles that Jack had brought them.

The little dogs, Frances, Gertrude, and Wilhelmina, were there too, curled up in their respective baskets, having already put themselves to bed.

Seeing Meg and Bea, the dogs barked and the children sprang to attention.

"Mama," Oscar said to Meg. "What are you doing here?"

"We've come to show you our finery before the ball begins," Meg said.

"Is that your new dress, Miss Layton?" Agatha asked, coming forward.

"It is." Bea spread out the lace-trimmed skirts for their perusal. "What do you think? Does it pass muster?"

"You look ever so pretty!" Charlotte said.

"Like a princess," little Delphia added. "And you too, Auntie Meg. Can I touch your brooch?"

Meg leaned down so the child could examine the opal-and-diamond pin.

Bea had no jewelry of her own. She'd declined Hannah's offer of a matching necklace and earrings, and Kate's of a pair of diamond hair combs. There were limits, even to make-believe.

"Is Uncle Jack going to dance with you?" Agatha asked Bea.

"I'm sure he'd like to dance," Bea said. "But his leg might not cooperate."

"You'll have plenty of other chances," Meg assured Bea.

Bea struggled to maintain her smile. "I'm sure we will."

Meg cocked her head. "Ah! There's the m-music," she said. "Miss Layton and I must hurry now."

Bidding the children goodnight, and promising to tell them all about the ball in the morning, Bea and Meg exited the nursery and made their way down the stairs. Music floated up from the ballroom, the sounds of the village players tuning up their instruments.

"It's very m-much a Maidenbridge affair," Meg said as they descended the steps. "Jack is beloved by the local people. They're eager to welcome him home—and to meet his betrothed."

Bea inwardly quailed at the prospect. Truth be told, she would rather the villagers had not come to meet her at all. As for Jack's parents—

But it was too late to turn back.

Jack and Ivo awaited them in the entry hall, both of them dressed in their evening blacks.

Bea had to remind herself to breathe. A difficult proposition, given the picture Jack presented in his flawlessly cut tailcoat and trousers, with his white waistcoat gleaming. Never had Bea seen him looking so polished and untouchable. She privately wondered if there was a level of handsomeness greater than outrageously handsome. If there was, Jack had certainly achieved it tonight.

When he saw Bea, a slow smile spread across his face. Her blood warmed in answer as he came to take her hand, assisting her down the last step. "Well," he said. "You've finally managed to render me speechless."

"You're speaking now," she pointed out.

Jack grinned. "I'm speechless on the inside."

"Ladies," Ivo said. "You're both visions." He took Meg's arm. Drawing her close, he whispered something in her ear.

Meg laughed softly in response.

Hannah and St. Clare appeared in the hall that led from the ballroom. Kate and Charles were with them. The gentlemen were in black-and-white eveningwear and the ladies in lush, large-skirted gowns of rose crepe (for Hannah) and mazarine blue silk (for Kate).

"The first guests are due any minute," Hannah said. "Shall we form the receiving line?"

"If Jack is ready to greet all his well-wishers," Ivo said.

Jack dropped a significant glance at his injured leg. "How many well-wishers are we talking about?"

"It's open house," St. Clare said. "We may be standing here all night."

"What my husband means," Hannah interjected, "is that the moment you've had enough, you may retire to the ballroom."

"Should we wait for Mama and Papa?" Kate asked.

"We're here!" a woman's voice called from the top of the stairs.

Bea looked up. For the third time that evening, she felt her courage slip.

Lord and Lady Allendale descended the steps, side-by-side. He was tall and commanding, and very like his three sons, save for the lines that creased his face and the silver that streaked his golden hair. And she was quite similar to her daughter, self-possessed and beautiful, with the same dark blue eyes, and the same lustrous mink tresses—though hers held plentiful strands of gray.

Her ladyship's attention went straight to her youngest son. Having marked him, her unerring gaze fell on Bea.

Bea's hand tightened reflexively on Jack's.

He gave her hand a reassuring squeeze in return before releasing it to greet his parents. "Mother, father," he said.

"Jack." Lady Allendale embraced him. "We looked for you when we arrived. Mrs. Kirby said you had gone into Maidenbridge."

Jack bent to return his mother's embrace. He was substantially taller than she was. "I had an errand to attend to," he said. "I'm sorry I wasn't here to meet you."

"You're here now, that's what's important." She kissed him. "I thank God you're home."

"I fear I'm a little worse for wear."

She drew back to look at him. "The operation was a success?"

"According to the surgeon. I'm reserving judgment until I can walk without aid of this." Jack tapped his cane. "I'm told it will take time."

"You have time now," Lord Allendale said, greeting Jack in turn. "An abundance of it."

"With no more threat of danger," Lady Allendale added. "Only peace and quiet, and plenty of fresh air."

Jack's mouth hitched. "How dull you make the countryside sound."

"Not for you, it seems." Lord Allendale turned his ice-gray gaze on Bea. "We're informed that you have returned with a diversion."

Lady Allendale looked at Bea too, her smile freezing on her lips. "Not a diversion, my love. A fiancée."

Bea's spine stiffened under their regard. She was no stranger to scrutiny. She'd been examined countless times by previous employers—dressed down, raked over, dismissed. This wasn't so very different.

Except that it was.

Jack was beside her, once again taking her hand. Her friend in truth, even if he wasn't her fiancé. And these were his parents. His *much-loved* parents. Bea wanted them to think well of her.

"Mother, father," Jack said. "Allow me to present Miss Beatrice Layton. Bea, these are my parents, Lord and Lady Allendale."

There was a brief silence. Bea had the sensation that everyone except for the earl and countess was holding their breath. And then—

"Miss Layton," Lady Allendale said. "We are very pleased to meet you."

"And very surprised," Lord Allendale added dryly. "But Jack wouldn't be Jack if he wasn't delivering us the unexpected."

Bea curtsied. "My lady. My lord. It is an honor."

Outside, the crunch of carriage wheels on the drive announced the arrival of the first of the guests. More carriage wheels sounded in quick succession, followed by the swell of voices as people disembarked from their conveyances and climbed the stone steps to the door. By the general noise, one would think it was a horde descending.

"We expect the whole of Maidenbridge," St. Clare said to his parents. "They're eager to welcome home the conquering hero."

Jack shot a warning look at his brother. "Enough of this hero nonsense. If this is to be a celebration, let it be for my engagement."

A trace of a smile edged St. Clare's mouth. "As you wish."

Hannah effortlessly guided the Beresfords into their receiving line. All except for Lady Allendale, who lingered for a moment longer in front of Bea.

"Hannah was wise to bring you here to Beasley," her ladyship said. "And to summon us all to join you. I mean for you and I to become better acquainted during your stay."

Bea's heart hammered. She didn't know how to reply. She wouldn't be staying after today. Tonight was the night she and Jack's fake engagement came to an end. That's what they'd agreed to.

She gave him a discreet glance, anticipating that he would be sharing her thoughts as he so often seemed to do. But Jack only smiled.

And then he winked at her.

# Chapter Twenty-Five

J ack sat back in his chair on the edge of the polished wood floor as the village musicians brought another country dance to a close.

The ballroom was as elegantly adorned and brilliantly lit as it had been during the countless other balls that had taken place at Beasley in his lifetime. He recalled creeping down the marble stairs to spy on the guests as a child in company with Ivo and Kate, all of them too young to attend the ball themselves. And then there were the balls at Beasley that Jack *had* been permitted to attend. The 20-piece orchestras, the blazing chandeliers, and the dances with comely widows, young wives, and local squires' daughters.

Jack had always been in demand.

He still was, much to his chagrin.

Despite the lure of the dancing, there were many who had chosen to remain in the chairs around him. Local gentlemen talking his ear off, and scores of Maidenbridge ladies bringing him punch as though he were an invalid. As the evening progressed, some of them had dissipated, leaving only the village's balding, middle-aged doctor and his kindly spinster daughter in attendance.

"A welcome home dinner might have been wiser," the doctor remarked from his chair beside Jack for what must be the tenth time. "You could have sat through the whole of it."

"Oh, but a ball is so joyous," the doctor's daughter declared. "And you don't mind not dancing, do you Colonel Beresford?"

Jack forced another smile. The truth was, he minded like the very devil. But not enough to damage his leg just as it was making a recovery. And not enough to embarrass himself, clinging to Bea in place of his cane as they shuffled through an approximation of a waltz.

*She* had been dancing since the opening set. First with Ivo, then with Charles, then with James. Even Jack's father had partnered her for a dance.

Jack couldn't tell if Bea was enjoying any of it. It was difficult to see her clearly in such a crush. He was grateful when the musicians played their final notes and the dancers at last withdrew from the floor.

Bea was among them, looking flushed and pretty in her low-cut fitted bodice and profusion of amber lace skirts.

Jack rose from his chair, resting his weight on his cane. "If you'll excuse me?" he said to the doctor and his daughter. "I've just spied my intended."

Taking his leave from them, he crossed the floor to meet Bea halfway.

Bea opened her fan as he approached, wafting her heated face. "It's rather close in here."

"Shall we repair to the terrace?" Jack asked. "Hannah's had the torches lit."

"That would be lovely," Bea said.

He offered her his arm and she took it. Together they made their way through the crowds toward the row of glass doors that led onto the ballroom terrace. Jack caught sight of his parents as they passed, along with James and Hannah. His mother and father had a knowing look in their eyes, and James was wearing the same smug smile he'd sported in the hall.

Jack's stomach coiled into a knot. Did all of his family know how he felt? What he intended? Was he that transparent?

Or perhaps it was only that James had learned where in the village Jack had gone today on his mysterious errand. And told the others too by the looks of it.

Yet, Bea didn't appear to have any inkling whatsoever. She walked through the terrace door ahead of him when he opened it for her, going straight to the stone rail. The rose gardens lay below, the winding paths through the beds lit with torches of their own. And above...

"An excessively starry night," Bea murmured.

Jack came to stand at her side. It was a cool evening, the darkness kept at bay by the flickering light of the torches that had been placed at opposite ends of the terrace. "More than the skies we saw from the Pera?"

"The stars seem brighter here."

"Everything does," he said. "I'd say our visit has been a success."

"Yes." She set her hands on the rail. A painted fan dangled from one slim wrist. Her bare shoulders rose and fell on a sigh. "But all good things must end eventually."

Jack didn't believe it. Not this good thing, anyway. "Meaning?"

"We have our amicable breakup to consider." She turned to him, one hand still resting on the stone railing. Her face was solemn in the torchlight. "We could do it publicly."

Jack wrinkled his brow, affecting to give the matter his due consideration. "A public breakup? Here?"

The strains of a waltz drifted from the ballroom.

"A quarrel or something," Bea said.

"What would you and I have to quarrel over?"

"I don't know," she said. "I suppose I could accuse you of meddling with village girls like you used to do."

Jack stifled a smile. He *had* mentioned that, hadn't he? It had been that day by the stream. He'd marked her reaction, albeit after the fact. "You'd have a difficult case to make."

"Would I?"

"They were meaningless stolen kisses," he said. "The last one I pilfered was from the blacksmith's daughter when I was one and twenty. There's been nothing since."

"Oh." Bea's forehead creased. "In that case—"

"You could claim indifference," Jack said.

An unidentifiable emotion crossed her face. "What?"

"You know, say you've fallen out of love with me. Or— even better—that you never loved me in the first place."

Bea's gaze slid from his. She resumed looking at the sky, her lips pressed in a frown. "I wonder," she said quietly, "how many more lies I must tell before all this is over?"

Jack's chest tightened. It was a lie, was it? To say she never loved him? That she didn't love him still? "Where is the lie in that?" he asked.

She cast him a bleak look. But she made no reply.

Jack's pulse quickened on a ridiculous surge of hope. He hadn't realized until this moment how anxious he'd been all evening. How dratted uncertain as he'd watched her dancing, all the while fearing that she was slipping away from him. That he'd lose his chance for happiness. That he'd lose *her*.

No battle he'd fought had been more worth winning. No stakes ever so high.

"It doesn't have to end tonight," he said abruptly.

Bea betrayed no reaction. "You propose our fake engagement continue? Until when this time? Until the end of your parents' visit? Until you move in to the Priory?" Bitterness crept into her words. "Or is this ruse to go on indefinitely? To save you from future pursuers, perhaps?"

"Don't be daft," Jack said. "I'm not *that* selfish. And I'm not proposing any of that. I'm simply..."

She looked at him fully. "What?"

He offered her a brief, lopsided smile. "Proposing."

Bea stared at him, frozen where she stood. The cool evening breeze whispered over her bare arms and throat, making gooseflesh rise on her skin. Her heart beat so heavily it was in her ears. She thought she hadn't heard him correctly.

Jack looked back at her steadily. A lock of blond hair had fallen forward over his brow. "By the way," he added, "it hasn't been a lie. None of it. Not since we docked at Southampton."

She shook her head. It wasn't true. It couldn't be.

Jack continued, explaining, "You asked me then if I meant to make my proposal in earnest."

"And you didn't answer," she reminded him. Her voice seemed to catch somewhere in her throat.

"I did," he said. "Not in words, perhaps but in the next moment, I was introducing you to my brother and sister-in-law as my fiancée. If that wasn't an answer—"

Her hand fell from the rail. She took a step back. "Don't do that. Don't make it out that you felt this way all along."

Jack caught her gently by the wrist, arresting her step. "Not all along," he said. "Not at first. It wasn't until after we formulated our plans that my feelings started to change."

Bea didn't understand him. Indeed, she didn't understand any of it. "Why?"

"*Why?* Because you're brave, principled, infuriatingly sensible, but with a keen sense of the ridiculous. Because you're beautiful—"

"I'm not."

"You are," he said with a trace of fierceness. "With your hair in its crown of plaits. With your gown muddy. With your eyes blazing as you faced down Mrs. Dimsdale and the rest of them."

Her throat convulsed on a swallow. "Jack..."

"I bought something for you today," he said. Releasing her wrist, he reached into the inner pocket of his tailcoat.

Bea watched, stunned, as he withdrew a small jeweler's box. He opened the lid to reveal the engagement ring within.

And her heart stopped. It simply stopped.

"This is where I was when my parents arrived," he said. "At a jeweler's shop in Maidenbridge, hoping against hope that the village would have something that might do you justice." Taking her hand, he slid the ring onto her finger.

It was a delicate band of gold, with a single, rose-cut diamond at its center. A *large* diamond.

"Oh my," Bea breathed.

Jack's expression softened. He cupped her face with his hand. His thumb brushed over the curve of her cheek. "Would it be so terrible to be Mrs. Jack Beresford?" he asked. "To give up your ambitions for a new position and throw in your lot with me at the Priory? As my wife?"

Tears stung at the back of her eyes as she lifted her gaze to his. "Not terrible," she whispered. "It would be a dream come true."

Jack's eyes blazed. "Then—"

"But not if you don't love me as I love you."

"I do love you, Bea," Jack said. "What do you think all this has been about?" And bending his head, his mouth captured hers.

Bea's eyes fell closed as her lips yielded to his. She brought her hands to his chest. They slid up to his shoulders as she kissed him back. Her pulse was surging, and her heart was as full as it had ever been. Full of hope and possibility. And love.

Never in her life had she dared to let herself feel so much. It hadn't been safe, during those long years on her own. To yearn for something—for *someone*—so specifically. Even her wishes had been general. All those lonely entreaties made on various evening stars. She'd only ever asked for something more.

But the stars had known the desires of her heart.

Someone up there had known.

Because here it was.

Here *he* was.

At length, Jack pulled back to look at her, his color high. He was smiling. "Shall I take that as a yes?" he asked.

She nodded, smiling back at him, even as her vision blurred with another prickle of joyful tears. "Yes."

Jack kissed her once more. "You *will* marry me?"

"Yes," she said again, laughing. "I will."

# Epilogue

*Eight months later...*

Christmases at Beasley Park had always been celebrated to the utmost, and this year was no exception. All of Jack's siblings and their families had come to stay. So had his parents. Hannah and Charles's parents, Arthur and Phyllida Heywood, were there too, having made the journey up from their Somerset estate a week early in order to spend more time with their children and grandchildren.

A towering Christmas tree dominated the drawing room. It was decorated with gilded fruit and nuts, and illuminated by dozens of small wax candles. Most of the children were on the carpeted floor around it, amid a pack of dozing dogs and a profusion of discarded wrapping paper and ribbons. They chattered and laughed with each other as they played with their new dolls, toy trains, and the hand-painted, eerily lifelike battalions of miniature soldiers that

Jack had commissioned for each of them on a recent trip to London.

"The girls too?" Bea had questioned when he'd placed the order.

"Especially the girls," Jack had replied. "Beresfords enjoy strategy. And we're none of us afraid of a fight."

Bea had only laughed. She wasn't afraid of a fight either, he knew. Not if the cause was just.

But it wasn't her courage that had most impressed Jack since their marriage. It was her softness. She'd already been revealing it to him by degrees before they'd wed. But since they had set up house at the Priory, since their days—and their nights—had proven so blissful, so fulfilling, the starchy façade Bea had hidden behind when first they'd met had all but vanished.

Jack understood why.

She was safe with him. Secure in her home, and in her happiness. And she trusted him absolutely.

A humbling fact.

Every day, Jack endeavored to deserve it. To be worthy of her friendship, her trust, her love. Given the glow in Bea's face and the lightness of her step as she moved through their new life together, he flattered himself that he was, in some small measure, succeeding.

"Your gifts to the children are always a success," she remarked from her place beside him on the overstuffed drawing-room sofa. Dressed in a green velvet gown, she held a glass of mulled wine in one hand. Her other hand was firmly in Jack's.

"Indeed," Kate agreed. "Jack's presents put the rest of us in the shade." She was seated near the crackling fire with her husband, holding her new baby in her arms—a little boy who had been christened George.

Jack idly moved his thumb over the back of Bea's knuckles as he replied to his sister. "You're not honestly comparing the effect of my humble wooden soldiers with that of a new pony?"

The cream-colored Shetland that Captain and Mrs. Heywood had bought their youngest granddaughter had arrived earlier that morning, with a red satin ribbon on its little arched neck and an engraved silver plate on its halter proclaiming its name: Sugar Plum. Charlotte had been ecstatic. So had the other children. It had taken a Herculean effort to get them all back to the house. Jack had ended up carrying two of his nephews in over his shoulders, thanking God that his leg had healed well enough that he could now get around tolerably well without his cane.

Kate pulled a face. "Point taken." She directed a look of mock severity at her in-laws. "It was the pony that eclipsed everything else."

"A grandparents' privilege," Captain Heywood replied with faint amusement. A tall, somber gentlemen, with graying black hair, he had served with distinction in the Peninsular Wars. He still walked with a stick on account of his injuries.

His wife, Phyllida, was next to him. She was a profoundly gentle lady, possessed of a striking feature: a pair of mismatched eyes, one blue and one brown. "We had no idea that the dear little creature would cause such a stir."

"It was a generous gift," James said graciously. He stood with Hannah near the fireplace, his arm around her waist.

"And a well-thought one," Hannah added. "It's past time Charlotte had a mount of her own."

"Very well thought," Jack's mother remarked wryly, sipping her wine. "One wonders how my husband and I are to compete?"

Mrs. Heywood smiled, no doubt recalling the lavish gifts Jack's parents had bestowed on the children in previous years. "It's not a competition, thank heaven."

"No, indeed," Jack's father replied. "I'm happy to say that our grandchildren want for nothing."

"We must take care not to spoil them," James said.

Jack scoffed at his brother. "We can surely spoil them a little today. It is Christmas after all."

"I shall spoil myself with all this gingerbread," Meg said, finishing her second piece. She was with Ivo on the settee, the two of them seated particularly close.

"You must eat," Ivo encouraged her. "It doesn't do to abstain in your condition."

Meg was expecting a child in the new year. She and Ivo had announced the good news last month, to everyone's delight.

Jack raised Bea's hand to his lips. He pressed a kiss to it. She smiled warmly at him in return. They had been the recipients of happy news of their own very recently. But it was too soon to share it. For now, it was their secret.

Across the drawing room, Jack's mother surveyed her children and grandchildren with a satisfied eye. "Another year nearly done," she said. "How gratified I am that you are all happily settled."

"And settled so near," Mrs. Heywood said.

Captain Heywood took his wife's hand. Their fingers twined together with intimate affection. "There's much to be said for the West Country. And Somerset in particular."

"I'll drink to that," Jack's father said.

James raised his glass. "To Somerset."

"And to Devon," Kate added, joining their toast. Her and Charles's estate, Satterthwaite Court, was located in the neighboring county.

"Hear, hear," Charles said. "To Somerset and Devon."

"To the West Country!" The Beresfords and Heywoods lifted their glasses.

As his family toasted, Jack raised his own glass to his wife in a private salute. "And to us, my love," he said softly.

Bea's porcelain blue eyes shone as she raised her glass to him in return. "To us, my darling," she said. "And to all the happiness to come."

# Author's Note

Way back in 2019 when I first published my novel *The Work of Art*, I never envisioned it being part of a series. Only after publishing my novel *Gentleman Jim* in 2020 did it occur to me that, in the entirety of my catalogue, only two of my books were set during the Regency era and that both of them took place in Somerset. It seemed to me that there was every chance the characters from those two novels might have met. Or, at the very least, that their children might have done.

This train of thought opened up so many possibilities to me, not only for additional stories, but for stories that I could write purely for fans of those first two novels.

Thus, the Somerset Stories series was born. Not as a formal series in its own right, but as a fan service. The novels are shorter, sweeter, and less complex than *The Work of Art* and *Gentleman Jim*, but for readers who loved those first two stories, these subsequent, second-generation books are a way of stepping back in and reconnecting with those characters and that world.

Speaking of reconnecting, in *The Governess and the Rogue*, the timeline didn't only match up for my Regency novels. It finally caught up with my Victorian ones. Since Bea was returning from India after the rebellion, it felt like the perfect time to give you all a peek at Justin Thornhill's journey home after his own experiences in India.

If you've read *The Matrimonial Advertisement* (Parish Orphans of Devon, Book 1) you'll know that Justin begins the novel as a gruff and rather grumpy battle-scarred former soldier. But in this book, you get to see how truly damaged he was when he first sailed back to England. You also get to see the two men that meet him at the docks. (Because what would one of my novels be if there wasn't a glimpse of, or a reference to, my intrepid lawyer hero and fixer Tom Finchley?)

It's been such a pleasure to bring these stories to you. It's also been rather difficult as I've had to balance writing them with my health issues, and with my publishing commitments for my Belles of London series and my Crinoline Academy series. Because of that, I was certain that Jack Beresford's book would be the last in my Somerset Stories universe.

And yet...

There was a spirited, animal-loving supporting character in this story who caught my imagination. A little girl I can all-too-easily picture as a heroine in a future novel. Perhaps, one day, I'll write her story.

# Acknowledgments

This book wouldn't have been possible without the support of my excellent team. Many thanks to my wonderful assistant and friend Rel Mollet; to my brilliant literary agent Kevan Lyon; to Kathryn Stuart, my very patient editor at Audible; to James Egan for cover design; to Anne Victory and Crystalle for edits and proofing; and to Alex Wyndham for his stellar work narrating all of my Somerset Stories novels.

Thanks, love, and gratitude are also due to my amazing mom, and to my devoted menagerie—Stella, Jet, Tavi, Bijou, and Asteria.

Last but never least, I'd like to thank you, my readers. I'm so grateful to you for sticking with me, and with this series. These second-generation stories were written entirely for you!

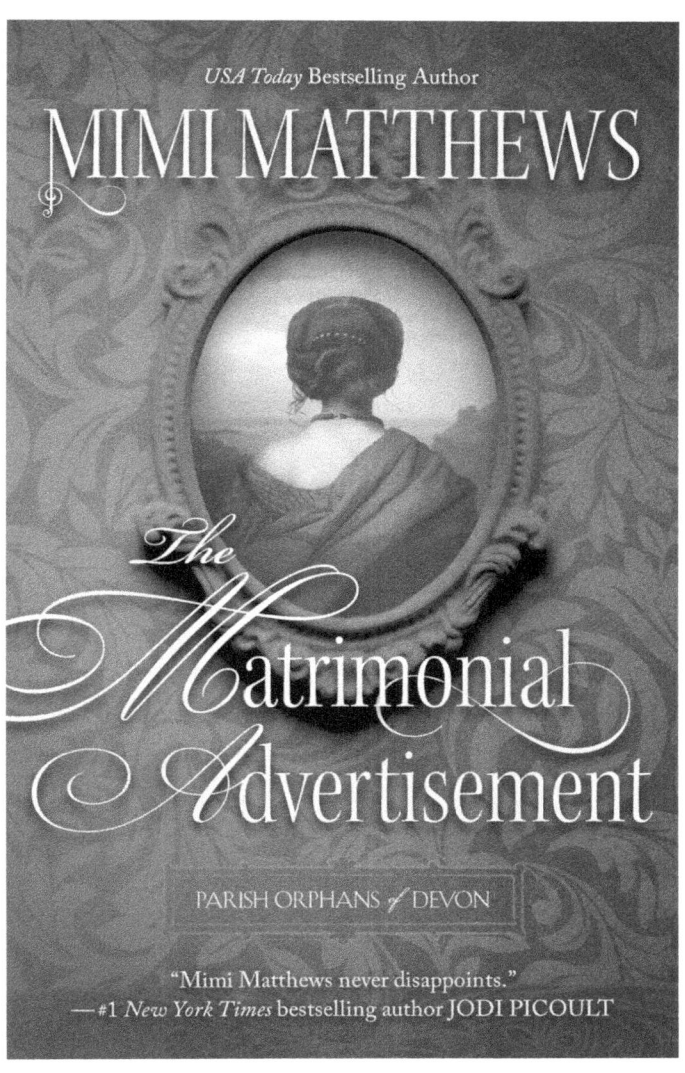

USA Today Bestselling Author

MIMI MATTHEWS

*The*
*Matrimonial*
*Advertisement*

PARISH ORPHANS *of* DEVON

"Mimi Matthews never disappoints."
—#1 *New York Times* bestselling author JODI PICOULT

Keep reading for a peek at the first book in Mimi
Matthews' acclaimed Parish Orphans of Devon series.
Available now.

## CHAPTER ONE

*North Devon, England*
*September 1859*

Helena Reynolds crossed the floor of the crowded taproom, her carpetbag clutched in her trembling hands. The King's Arms was only a small coaching inn on the North Devon coast road, but it seemed to her as if every man in Christendom had gathered there to have a pint. She could feel their eyes on her as she navigated carefully through their midst. Some stares were merely curious. Others were openly assessing.

She suppressed a shiver. She was hardly dressed for seduction in her gray striped-silk traveling gown, though she'd certainly made an effort to look presentable. After all, it was not every day that one met one's future husband.

"Can I help you, ma'am?" the innkeeper called to her from behind the crowded bar.

"Yes. If you please, sir." Tightening her hands on her carpetbag, she approached the high counter. A very tall man was leaning against the end of it, nursing his drink. His lean, muscular frame was shrouded in a dark wool greatcoat, his face partially hidden by his upturned collar and a tall beaver hat tipped low over his brow. She squeezed into the empty space beside him, her heavy petticoats and crinoline rustling loudly as they pressed against his leg.

She lowered her voice to address the innkeeper directly. "I'm here to see—"

"Blevins!" a man across the room shouted. "Give us another round!"

Before Helena could object, the innkeeper darted off to oblige his customers. She stared after him in helpless frustration. She'd been expected at one o'clock precisely. And now, after the mix-up at the railway station and the delay with the accommodation coach—she cast an anxious glance at the small watch she wore pinned to the front of her bodice—it was already a quarter past two.

"Sir!" she called to the innkeeper. She stood up on the toes of her half boots, trying to catch his eye. "Sir!"

He did not acknowledge her. He was exchanging words with the coachman at the other end of the counter as he filled five tankards with ale. The two of them were laughing together with the ease of old friends.

Helena gave a soft huff of annoyance. She was accustomed to being ignored, but this was the outside of enough. Her whole life hinged on the next few moments.

She looked around for someone who might assist her. Her eyes fell at once on the gentleman at her side. He didn't appear to be a particularly friendly sort of fellow, but his height was truly commanding and surely he must have a voice to match his size.

"I beg your pardon, sir." She touched him lightly on the arm with one gloved hand. His muscles tensed beneath her fingers. "I'm sorry to disturb you, but would you mind very much to summon—"

He raised his head from drinking and, very slowly, turned to look at her.

The words died on Helena's lips.

He was burned. Badly burned.

"Do you require something of me, ma'am?" he asked in an excruciatingly civil undertone.

She stared up at him, her first impression of his appearance revising itself by the second. The burns, though severe, were limited to the bottom right side of his face, tracing a path from his cheek down to the edge of his collar and beyond it, she was sure. The rest of his face—a stern face with a strongly chiseled jaw and hawklike aquiline nose—was relatively unmarked. Not only unmarked, but with his black hair and smoke-gray eyes, actually quite devastatingly handsome.

"Do you require something of me?" he asked again, more sharply this time.

She blinked. "Yes. Do forgive me. Would you mind very much summoning the innkeeper? I cannot seem to—"

"*Blevins!*" the gentleman bellowed.

The innkeeper broke off his loud conversation and scurried back to their end of the counter. "What's that, guv?"

"The lady wishes to speak with you."

"Thank you, sir," Helena said. But the gentleman had already turned his attention back to his drink, dismissing her without a word.

"Yes, ma'am?" the innkeeper prompted.

Abandoning all thoughts of the handsome—and rather rude—stranger at her side, Helena once again addressed herself to the innkeeper. "I was supposed to meet someone here at one o'clock. A Mr. Boothroyd?" She felt the gentleman next to her stiffen, but she did not regard it. "Is he still here?"

"Another one for Boothroyd, are you?" The innkeeper looked her up and down. "Don't look much like the others."

Helena's face fell. "Oh?" she asked faintly. "Have there been others?"

"Aye. Boothroyd's with the last one now."

"The *last* one?" She couldn't believe it. Mr. Boothroyd had given her the impression that she was the only woman with whom Mr. Thornhill was corresponding. And even if she wasn't, what sort of man interviewed potential wives for his employer in the same manner one might interview applicants for a position as a maidservant or a cook? It struck her as being in extraordinarily bad taste.

Was Mr. Thornhill aware of what his steward was doing?

She pushed the thought to the back of her mind. It was far too late for doubts. "As that may be, sir, I've come a very long way and I'm certain Mr. Boothroyd will wish to see me."

In fact, she was not at all certain. She had only ever met Mr. Finchley, the sympathetic young attorney in London. It was he who had encouraged her to come to Devon. While the sole interaction she'd had with Mr. Boothroyd and Mr. Thornhill thus far were letters—letters which she currently had safely folded within the contents of her carpetbag.

"Reckon he might at that," the innkeeper mused.

"Precisely. Now, if you'll inform Mr. Boothroyd I've arrived, I would be very much obliged to you."

The man beside her finished his ale in one swallow and then slammed the tankard down on the counter. "I'll take her to Boothroyd."

Helena watched, wide-eyed, as he stood to his full, towering height. When he glared down at her, she offered him a tentative smile. "I must thank you again, sir. You've been very kind."

He glowered. "This way." And then, without a backward glance, he strode toward the hall.

Clutching her carpetbag tightly, she trotted after him.

Her heart was skittering, her pulse pounding in her ears. She prayed she wouldn't faint before she'd even submitted to her interview.

The gentleman rapped once on the door to the private parlor. It was opened by a little gray-haired man in spectacles. He peered up at the gentleman, frowned, and then, with furrowed brow, looked past him to stare at Helena herself.

"Mr. Boothroyd?" she queried.

"I am Boothroyd," he said. "And you, I presume, are Miss Reynolds?"

"Yes, sir. I know I'm dreadfully late for my appointment..." She saw a woman rising from a chair within the private parlor. A woman who regarded Helena with an upraised chin, her face conveying what words could not. "Oh," Helena whispered. And just like that it seemed the tiny, flickering flame of hope she'd nurtured these last months blinked out. "You've already found someone else."

"As to that, Miss Reynolds—" Mr. Boothroyd broke off with an expression of dismay as the tall gentleman brushed past him to enter the private parlor. He removed his hat and coat and proceeded to take a seat by the raging fire in the hearth.

The woman gaped at him in dismay. "Mr. Boothroyd!" she hissed, hurrying to the older gentleman's side. "I thought this was a *private* parlor."

"So it is, Mrs. Standish." Mr. Boothroyd consulted his pocket watch. "Or was, until half an hour ago. Never mind it. Our interview is finished in any case. Now, if you would be so good as to..."

Helena didn't hear the rest of their conversation. All she could hear was the sound of her own beating heart. She didn't know why she remained. She'd have to board the coach and continue to Cornwall. And then what? Fling herself from the cliffs, she supposed. There was no other way. Oh, what a fool she'd been to think this would work in the first place! If only Jenny had never seen that advertisement in the paper. Then she would have known months ago that there was but one means of escape from this wretched tangle. She would never have had reason to hope!

Her vision clouded with tears. She turned from the private parlor, mumbling an apology to Mr. Boothroyd as she went.

"Miss Reynolds?" Mr. Boothroyd called. "Have you changed your mind?"

She looked back, confused, only to see that the other lady was gone and that Mr. Boothroyd stood alone in the entryway. From his seat by the fire, the tall gentleman ruffled a newspaper, seeming to be wholly unconcerned with either of them. "No, sir," she said.

"If you will have a seat." He gestured to one of the chairs that surrounded a small supper table. On the table was a stack of papers and various writing implements. She watched him rifle through them as she took a seat. "I trust you had a tolerable journey."

"Yes, thank you."

"You took the train from London?"

"I did, sir, but only as far as Barnstaple. Mr. Finchley arranged for passage on an accommodation coach to bring me the rest of the way here. It's one of the reasons I'm late. There was an overturned curricle in the road. The coachman stopped to assist the driver."

"One of the reasons, you say?"

"Yes, I...I missed the earlier train at the station," she

confessed. "I'd been waiting at the wrong platform and...by the time I realized my error, my train had already gone. I was obliged to change my ticket and take the next one."

"Have you no maid with you? No traveling companion?"

"No, sir. I traveled alone." There hadn't been much choice. Jenny had to remain in London, to conceal Helena's absence as long as possible. Helena had considered hiring someone to accompany her, but there'd been no time and precious little money to spare. Besides which, she didn't know who she could trust.

Mr. Boothroyd continued to sift through his papers. Helena wondered if he was even listening to her. "Ah. Here it is," he said at last. "Your initial reply to the advertisement." He withdrew a letter covered in small, even handwriting which she recognized as her own. "As well as a letter from Mr. Finchley in London with whom you met on the fifteenth." He perused a second missive with a frown.

"Is anything the matter?" she asked.

"Indeed. It says here that you are five and twenty." Mr. Boothroyd lowered the letter. "You do not look five and twenty, Miss Reynolds."

"I assure you that I am, sir." She began to work at the ribbons of her gray silk traveling bonnet. After untying the knot with unsteady fingers, she lifted it from her head, twined the ribbons round it, and placed it atop her carpetbag. When she raised her eyes, she found Mr. Boothroyd staring at her. "I always look much younger in a bonnet. But, as you can see now, I'm—"

"Young *and* beautiful," he muttered with disapproval.

She blushed, glancing nervously at the gentleman by the fire. He did not seem to be listening, thank goodness. Even so, she leaned forward in her chair, dropping her voice. "Does Mr. Thornhill not want a pretty wife?"

"This isn't London, Miss Reynolds. Mr. Thornhill's house is isolated. Lonely. He seeks a wife who can bear the solitude. Who can manage his home and see to his comforts. A sturdy, capable sort of woman. Which is precisely why the advertisement specified a preference for a widow or spinster of more mature years."

"Yes, but I—"

"What Mr. Thornhill doesn't want," he continued, "is a starry-eyed girl who dreams of balls and gowns and handsome suitors. A marriage with such a frivolous creature would be a recipe for disaster."

Helena bristled. "That isn't fair, sir."

"Excuse me?"

"I'm no starry-eyed girl. I never was. And with respect, Mr. Boothroyd, you haven't the slightest notion of my dreams. If I wanted balls and gowns or...or frivolous things...I'd never have answered Mr. Thornhill's advertisement."

"What exactly do you seek out of this arrangement, Miss Reynolds?"

She clasped her hands tightly in her lap to stop their trembling. "Security," she answered honestly. "And perhaps...a little kindness."

"You couldn't find a gentleman who met these two requirements in London?"

"I don't wish to be in London. Indeed, I wish to be as far from London as possible."

"You friends and family...?"

"I'm alone in the world, sir."

"I see."

Helena doubted that very much. "Mr. Boothroyd, if you've already decided someone else is better suited—"

"There is no one else, Miss Reynolds. At present, you're the only lady Mr. Finchley has recommended."

"But the woman who was here before—"

"Mrs. Standish?" Mr. Boothroyd removed his spectacles. "She was applying for the position of housekeeper at the Abbey." He rubbed the bridge of his nose. "Regrettably, we have an ongoing issue with retaining adequate staff. It's something you should be aware of if you intend to take up residence."

She exhaled slowly. "A housekeeper. Of course. How silly of me. Mr. Thornhill mentioned the difficulties you were having with servants in one of his letters."

"I'm afraid it's proven quite a challenge." Mr. Boothroyd settled his spectacles back on his nose. "Not only is the house isolated, it has something of a local reputation. Perhaps you've heard...?"

"A little. But Mr. Finchley told me it was nothing more than ignorant superstition."

"Quite so. However, in this part of the world, Miss Reynolds, you'll find ignorance is in ready supply."

Helena was unconcerned. "I should like to see the Abbey for myself."

"Yes, yes. All in good time."

"And I should like to meet Mr. Thornhill."

"Undoubtedly." Mr. Boothroyd shuffled through his papers again. To her surprise, a rising color crept into the elderly man's face. "There are just one or two more points at issue, Miss Reynolds." He cleared his throat. "You're aware, I presume... That is, I do hope Mr. Finchley explained...this marriage is to be a real marriage in every sense of the word."

She looked at him, brows knit in confusion. "What other kind of marriage would it be?"

"And you're agreeable?"

"Of course."

He made no attempt to disguise his skepticism. "There are many ladies who would find such an arrangement singularly lacking in romance."

Helena didn't doubt it. She'd have balked at the prospect herself once. But much had changed in the past year—and in the past months, especially. Any girlish fantasies she'd harbored about true love were dead. In their place was a rather ruthless pragmatism.

"I don't seek romance, Mr. Boothroyd. Only kindness. And Mr. Finchley said that Mr. Thornhill was a kind man."

Mr. Boothroyd appeared to be surprised by this. "Did he indeed," he murmured. "What else did he tell you, pray?"

She hesitated before repeating the words that Mr. Finchley had spoken. Words that had convinced her once and for all to travel to a remote coastal town in Devon, to meet and marry a complete stranger. "He told me that Mr. Thornhill had been a soldier, and that he knew how to keep a woman safe."

Justin Thornhill cast another brooding glance at the pale, dark-haired beauty sitting across from Boothroyd. She was slight but shapely, her modest traveling gown doing nothing to disguise the high curve of her breasts and the narrow lines of her small waist. When first he'd seen her in the taproom, he thought she was a fashionable traveler on her way to

Abbot's Holcombe, the resort town farther up the coast. He had no reason to think otherwise. The Miss Reynolds he'd been expecting—the plain, sensible spinster who'd responded to his matrimonial advertisement—had never arrived.

This Miss Reynolds was a different class of woman altogether.

She sat across from Boothroyd, her back ramrod straight, and her elegant, gloved hands folded neatly on her lap in a pretty attitude. She regarded the curmudgeonly steward with wide, doelike hazel eyes and when she spoke, she did so in the smooth, cultured tones of a gentlewoman. No, Justin amended. Not a gentlewoman. A *lady*.

She was nothing like the two sturdy widows Boothroyd had interviewed earlier for the position of housekeeper. Those women had, ironically, been more in line with Justin's original specifications—the specifications he had barked at his aging steward those many months ago when Boothroyd had first broached the idea of his advertising for a wife.

"I have no interest in courtship," he'd said, "nor in weeping young ladies who take to their bed with megrims. What I need is a woman. A woman who is bound by law and duty to see to the running of this godforsaken mausoleum. A woman I can bed on occasion. Damnation, Boothroyd, I didn't survive six years in India so I could live like a bloody monk when I returned home."

They were words spoken in frustration after the last in a long line of housekeepers had quit without notice. Words that owed a great deal to physical loneliness and far too many glasses of strong spirits.

The literal-minded Boothroyd had taken them as his marching orders.

The next morning, before Justin had even arisen from his alcohol-induced slumber, his ever-efficient steward had arranged for an advertisement to be placed in the London papers. It had been brief and to the point:

*MATRIMONY: Retired army officer, thirty-two, of moderate means and quiet disposition wishes to marry a spinster or widow of the same age. Suitable lady will be sensible, compassionate, and capable of managing the household of remote country property. Independent fortune unimportant. Letters to be addressed, postpaid, to Mr. T. Finchley, Esq., Fleet Street.*

Justin had initially been angry. He'd even threatened to give Boothroyd the sack. However, within a few days he'd found himself warming to the idea of acquiring a wife by advertisement. It was modern and efficient. As straightforward as any other business transaction. The prospective candidates would simply write to Thomas Finchley, Justin's London attorney, and Finchley would negotiate the rest, just as competently as he'd negotiated the purchase of Greyfriar's Abbey or those shares Justin had recently acquired in the North Devon Railway.

Still, he had no intention of making the process easy. He'd informed both Boothroyd and Finchley that he would not bestir himself on any account. If a prospective bride wanted to meet, she would have to do so at a location within easy driving distance of the Abbey.

He'd thought such a condition would act as a deterrent.

It hadn't occurred to him that women routinely traveled

such distances to take up employment. And what was his matrimonial advertisement if not an offer for a position in his household?

In due time, Finchley had managed to find a woman for whom an isolated existence in a remote region of coastal Devon sounded agreeable. Justin had even exchanged a few brief letters with her. Miss Reynolds hadn't written enough for him to form a definite picture of her personality, nor of her beauty—or lack thereof. Nevertheless, he'd come to imagine her as a levelheaded spinster. The sort of spinster who would endure his conjugal attentions with subdued dignity. A spinster who wouldn't burst into tears at the sight of his burns.

The very idea that anything like this lovely young creature would grace his table and his bed was frankly laughable.

Not but that she wasn't determined.

Though that was easily remedied. Folding his paper, Justin rose from his chair. "I'll take it from here, Boothroyd."

Miss Reynold's eyes lifted to his. He could see the exact moment when she realized who he was. To her credit, she didn't cry or faint or spring from her chair and bolt out of the room. She merely looked at him in that same odd way she had in the taproom when first she beheld his burns.

"Miss Reynolds," Mr. Boothroyd said, "may I present Mr. Thornhill?"

**Add this title on Goodreads
or order today from your favorite store.**

# About the Author

*USA Today* bestselling author Mimi Matthews writes both historical nonfiction and award-winning proper Victorian romances. Her novels have received starred reviews in *Publishers Weekly*, *Library Journal*, *Booklist*, *Kirkus*, *Book-Page*, and *Shelf Awareness*, and her articles have been featured on the *Victorian Web*, *the Journal of Victorian Culture*, and in syndication at *BUST Magazine*. In her other life, Mimi is an attorney. She resides in California with her family, which includes an Andalusian dressage horse, a miniature poodle, a Sheltie, and two Siamese cats.

Connect Online
MimiMatthews.com
Facebook: @MimiMatthewsAuthor
Instagram: @MimiMatthewsEsq

www.ingramcontent.com/pod-product-compliance
Ingram Content Group UK Ltd.
Pitfield, Milton Keynes, MK11 3LW, UK
UKHW010711050825
7235UKWH00027B/231

9 798999 374707